BANG! YOU'RE DEAD

WATERFELL TWEED COZY MYSTERY SERIES:
BOOK FIVE

MONA MARPLE

For my Dad:
I miss you.

1

Sandy beamed at the sight of the familiar landscape of Waterfell Tweed revealed in front of her, finally. She stifled a yawn and then shook her head, opening her eyes wide as Tom slowed the car outside her cottage.

"Keep going." She said, with a glance across the car to him. His face was ashen with exhaustion. "Park up outside The Tweed and I'll walk back."

"Don't be silly." He said. His words slurred, vowels crashing into each other.

"Oh, come on. It's still light, and a bit of fresh air would be nice. Please?" She asked. The truth was, she didn't want Tom driving alone while he was so tired. She had made it her mission for the last twenty minutes, since drowsiness had taken him, to entertain him as much as possible. Her inane conversation was even driving herself mad, but it had kept him awake.

"Okay." He agreed. He indicated and moved on, and Sandy gazed out of the window at her familiar cottage.

"Did I ever tell you why I like bagels so much?" Sandy

asked. Tom managed a slight smile at the silly question. "In my opinion, it's a conversation you can't have too many times anyway. So, here's the thing with bagels. They make everything better. Cheese on toast? Try it on a bagel instead. Smashed avocado with a little chilli and plenty of black pepper? Delicious on a bagel."

Tom nodded but didn't answer, his focus fixed on the winding country road that led to the village square.

It was approaching 6pm and they were the only ones on the road. The fields on either side, secured by ancient dry stone walls, were lush with the promise of spring. A flock of sheep grazed on the hilltop, bellies bulging with lambs ready to be born. The shepherd, a man called Gurdip, stood close by, his faithful border collie sat by his side.

"You've gone quiet on me." Tom said from the driver seat.

"Oh no! Sorry, Tom, I guess I'm easily distracted." Sandy said. As she returned her attention to him she saw that the sight of home had reinvigorated him. His eyes were wider, and a smile was on his face. "You look brighter."

"It's good to be home." He said. "What were you looking at?"

"The shepherd's up there with his flock." Sandy explained. "It just looked like such a peaceful life, wandering around the fields with your sheep and your dog."

"Hmm." Tom said doubtfully. "I'm guessing you've never been a shepherd?"

Sandy laughed. "Well, no, but I'm fairly sure you haven't either!"

"Definitely not. Gurdip comes in the pub sometimes, though. I don't think you'd find many people with harder jobs in this village."

Sandy glanced back out of her window but the hilltop

had disappeared, swallowed by larger hills and the twist of the road.

"I guess it's like the people who look at my job and think all I do is cut slices of cake for people all day, with no worries greater than what colour apron to wear each day!" Sandy said, although she could never be too annoyed at the people with that opinion as she herself had expected owning a cafe and bookshop to be glamorous and fun.

"Everyone thinks other people have it easier than they do." Tom said. They were on the final approach to the village. Sandy could see a queue of people stood outside The Village Fryer, waiting for their evening fish and chips.

"I love this place." Sandy said. Contentment washed over her and she reached for Tom's hand that rested on the gear stick and gave it a small squeeze.

"Me too." He replied. "I've come to life a bit now, do you want to come in for a drink?"

Sandy shook her head. "I'm going to head home and see the cat. I'm looking forward to the walk."

"You really need to give that cat a name." Tom said. He parked outside The Tweed and turned the engine off, then turned to look at her. The colour had begun to return to his face.

"I've been thinking about that." Sandy admitted. "I'm going to have a chat with him when I get home."

"See which one he says yes to?"

"He's got a real personality, Tom. I think I'll know when I've found the right name for him. Anyway, you need to get off to bed. Thank you for coming with me, and doing the driving, I..."

"I've loved it, Sand." Tom said. "I'll follow you anywhere, okay?"

Sandy felt her cheeks flush at his words. "Let's just stay here for a while, yeah? The world is nice, but this is home."

"I couldn't agree more." Tom said. They climbed out of the car and she walked around to the pavement, where he pulled her in for an embrace. He planted a kiss on her forehead. "Text me when you get home?"

"I will, but I think you'll be asleep by then."

"Good point." He said with a laugh. She walked away, with a turn back once to see that he was on the doorstep of The Tweed watching her go. She raised an arm to give him a wave and he mimicked the gesture, then walked indoors.

The walk back to her cottage would take around twenty minutes, and although the sun was out, there was a chill in the air. Sandy zipped her yellow rain mac up and adjusted her scarf so it covered her throat and chin, and resisted the temptation to pull out her mobile phone and send messages informing people that she was home. She wanted to enjoy the scenery with her full attention.

"Evening, Sandy." A gentleman called from the chip shop queue. He was a regular face in Books and Bakes but Sandy didn't think she had ever known his name. If she had, she couldn't remember it.

"Hello!" She called in enthusiastic reply. A break in the wider world, where she was unknown, made her treasure village life and the fact that everyone knew her.

She continued walking, past the last shops of the village square and out into the glorious Peak District countryside.

She looked out for Gurdip and his sheep but dusk was approaching and she guessed they had all returned to the safety of the indoors.

Near her house, she spotted a small cluster of daffodils and smiled to herself.

"You know that Spring has sprung when you see

daffodils." She whispered as a huge smile took over her face.

As she walked up the path to her stone cottage, she felt the physical sensation of returning home. Her chest grew warm, her stomach flipped with excitement, and she had to restrain herself from running down the path.

Her key fit perfectly in the door, in a way she had never noticed or appreciated before.

The cottage was warm and the smell of an open fire greeted her. She closed the door after herself and padded through to the living room, where the crackle of embers burning in her coal fire welcomed her. A card sat on the coffee table, her name scrawled on the envelope.

She inhaled the rich woody scent of the fire deeply and opened the envelope.

Welcome home, Sandy. I asked Coral to have the cottage ready for your return. Stay warm, and I can't wait to see you next.
With love, Tom

Sandy grinned at the card, then remembered Tom's request.

She pulled the mobile phone out of her handbag and punched in a quick message thanking him for his kindness. She'd never been treated so well, and she could certainly get used to it.

"Right, where are you cat?" She called. She walked through the cottage, noticing the other things that Tom must have instructed Coral to do. In the kitchen, she found a bunch of daffodils in a vase on the small table, but no cat. In the fridge, where she hadn't expected the cat to be, she found an overflowing supply of her favourite foods. Back in the living room, on closer inspection, she saw that a pair of her most fluffy socks had been left to warm up by the fire, and took off the walking socks she was wearing and replaced them with the toasty warm pair, but didn't see the cat. In the bathroom, a new hot pink bath bomb sat waiting for her use, but there was no cat.

Finally, in her bedroom, she saw fresh, clean bedding, and the cat curled up on her pillow. He eyed her as she walked in, then closed his eyes again.

"Hello, you." Sandy said as she took a seat on the bed beside the cat. She reached out a hand and stroked his thick, black fur, and thought how nice it was to have company to return home to.

"We need to have a talk." She said. The cat opened one eye and watched her. "You need a name and we're not going to leave this room until we've agreed on one. I'll listen to your input, okay?"

The cat opened both eyes.

"Good, I have your attention. How about Snowflake? It's ironic because, you know, you're not white."

The cat closed his eyes and covered his face with a paw.

"Are you sure?" Sandy asked. "I thought that was a sassy name, like your personality. Okay then, do you like Boris?"

The cat played dead.

"Samuel?"

"How about Mr?" Sandy asked. "It's very respectful to call someone Mr."

The cat buried his head further underneath his paw.

"Tigger? Dennis? Hercules?"

The cat peered at her, let out a sneeze in her direction, and then returned to his previous pose.

"You could help, you know, instead of just reject my ideas." Sandy said. "How about Mull? I had a lovely time, by the way. Well, apart from one day, but I won't bore you with all of that. Anyway, not Mull, no, how about Frederick?"

The cat had begun to snore.

"Sleepy?" Sandy asked. "Sir Sleeps a Lot? Mr Snooze? I've got it, how about The Curious Incident of the Cat in My Bed? A bit long? I agree."

The cat opened one eye, seemed disappointed to see she was still there, and turned the other way.

"I've missed you too, you know." Sandy said. "Goodness, what am I doing talking to a cat? When did I become a crazy cat lady?"

The cat gave no reply.

"If you won't help me, you'll just be the cat forever." Sandy said. The cat turned to her, his eyes bright and keen, and padded across the bed, where he stood his back legs on her thighs and his front legs on her chest, so his face was close to her own.

"Meow." He said.

"Well, hello. This is nice. Hold on, is this you telling me you want to be The Cat?" Sandy asked.

The cat nestled his head on her chest and let out a soft purr.

"Okay, The Cat it is. I like it. It's a name for a regal animal with attitude, and that's you all over. The Cat. Very good." Sandy said.

The cat fell into a deep sleep on her chest, and his soft breathing was so peaceful she didn't want to disturb him. She felt her own eyes close and decided not to fight against it. She was home. She was safe.

In the morning, she would wake early and be the first to arrive at Books and Bakes. She loved the early morning time when nobody else was around, and she wanted to be there to greet her team as they each arrived for work. She would wake early and do all of the chores she had planned to do that evening.

Yes, tomorrow she would be productive. Tomorrow she would wake with a burst of energy and she would race through her to do list.

Tomorrow.

Now, she would close her eyes, and drift off to sleep.

2

*B*ooks and Bakes smelt of coconut and cleaning products when Sandy let herself in at just before 7am the next day.

She gazed around at her beloved cafe, from the wiped-down tables to the empty display counter, and a contented smile took over her face.

"Hello, you." Bernice's familiar voice came as the front door opened, a gust of wind coming in with her and making Sandy shiver.

Sandy turned to her friend and employee and scooped her in a hug, which Bernice allowed but didn't encourage. "I've missed you!"

"We've missed you too. This place isn't the same without your face and that monstrosity." Bernice said, as she extracted herself awkwardly from the embrace.

"This?" Sandy said. She looked down at her yellow rain mac. "It's the height of fashion, you know. Everyone's wearing them."

"Hmm." Bernice said. She was dressed in a much more muted wardrobe; her coat, trousers and ankle boots were all plain black. Her auburn hair was usually the main splash of colour on her, and it was such beautiful hair that it deserved to hold centre stage.

"How have things been here?" Sandy asked. "It's so nice to be back. Have you managed?"

"Of course." Bernice said. "We like you being around, Sand, but we can manage on our own."

"I know, I just worry..."

"Sounds like you had enough to worry about in Mull."

Sandy shook her head. "It was awful."

"Hopefully that's your share of murders done with now, eh? Let's keep your focus right here where it belongs." Bernice said. She had pulled on her apron and was about to walk through into the kitchen, when she turned and glanced at Sandy. "How's lover boy?"

Sandy felt her cheeks flush but allowed a grin to cross her lips. "I haven't spoken to him today. He was so tired yesterday, with the drive. Bless him."

"You've got it bad." Bernice teased. "Look at you, you're red like a beetroot!"

Sandy shifted uncomfortably from one foot to the other. "It's probably going from the cold to the warm in here..."

"Oh get, don't be daft. I'm only teasing you. You enjoy it, Sand. We all know you deserve a nice fella." Bernice said, and with that she retreated into the kitchen, where Sandy heard doors being opened and closed as she fetched ingredients to begin the day's baking.

Sandy walked through the seating area and climbed the stairs at the rear of the cafe. Her beloved bookshop upstairs was in darkness, and she flicked the light switch and felt her stomach flip as row after row of book case was revealed to her.

The gaps on the bookcases were even wider than they

had been before she left for her trip to Mull, which suggested that sales had continued to be high. The new stock bought from the Isle of Mull would be delivered any day to replenish the shelves.

Sandy could hardly wait to hide herself away upstairs, catalogueing and arranging the new stock. She planned to make herself a large mug of creamy, hot mocha to sip as she worked and set an incense stick to burn.

She walked through the upstairs space, inspecting each bookshelf quickly in turn.

The horticultural section looked bare and in need of fresh stock, and the military history section had been almost eviscerated in her time away. The small section that she allowed to be filled with popular fiction bulged as always, ignored by the book lovers who travelled to Books and Bakes for more specialist titles.

Sandy noted at least four copies of the country's current most popular novel, a book she had read and enjoyed despite lukewarm critic reviews, and wondered whether to get rid of the section entirely. It would give space for her to extend another, more in-demand area.

"Sandy!" A shriek came from downstairs, pulling Sandy away from her book bliss thoughts and back to reality.

She returned the yellowed book of poetry to the shelf where it should be, after retrieving it from the biography section, and made her way downstairs, two steps at a time.

Dorie Slaughter stood at the cafe counter, her hair dyed a new shade of bright orange, squeezed into a leopard print coat. Bernice, stood behind the counter with her arms folded across her chest, met Sandy's gaze and rolled her eyes. Bernice did not tolerate village gossip well and was happiest left undisturbed in the kitchen.

"Dorie?" Sandy enquired. "What's wrong?"

"Thank goodness you're back!" Dorie said. She spun on her kitten heels to face Sandy, her face red, eyes keen with information that she was hungry to share. "This village is going to the dogs. We need you to sort it out, Sandy."

"Sort what out?" Sandy asked.

"The murders!" Dorie exclaimed.

"She has sorted the murders out." Bernice said. "They'd still be looking for all the killers if it wasn't for Sandy."

"Not those murders!" Dorie cried.

"Get to the point, Dorie. What are you talking about?"

"You mean you haven't heard?" Dorie asked. A smile crept across her face. Dorie's favourite thing was breaking news to other people. Sandy had no doubt that whatever she had heard, she had sprinted to Books and Bakes to make sure she was the first to announce to other people. "Well, why didn't you say? Bernice, get me a bacon sandwich, I've been rushed off my feet and I need breakfast."

"We're not open yet." Bernice mumbled, but she walked back into the kitchen anyway and the sound of hot, sizzling oil soon followed.

"What's happened, Dorie?"

"I can't think without a mug of tea, be a dear and make me one?" Dorie asked. She sat at the table in the middle of the seating area, no doubt positioning herself for a full morning of breaking news to the other customers.

"Of course." Sandy said. She was so pleased to be home in Waterfell Tweed that Dorie's antics were a source of fond affection for her, nothing more. Her mention of murders concerned Sandy, as there was nothing she wanted to tackle less than another killing, but Dorie was often more dramatic than she needed to be. There was every chance the news would turn out to be the library changing their opening hours or something similarly mundane.

Sandy allowed her mind to wander to the days she had spent with Tom Nelson in the Isle of Mull, and how much she had enjoyed his company. She should text him, as soon as she got chance, to thank him again for his company and driving.

"Here you go." Sandy said. She placed the large mug of weak tea in front of Dorie, who inspected the colour of the drink and nodded her approval.

"You never forget how I like my tea." She complimented Sandy. "I thought now you're loved up and a big-wig, you'd forget the little details."

"Never." Sandy assured her. "And I'm hardly a big-wig. Now, what's this news?"

"We need to wait for Bernice." Dorie said.

"You really don't." Bernice said. She appeared at the table and placed Dorie's food in front of her. Three thick rashers of bacon sat on a sandwich of white, doorstep bread smothered in salted butter. The sight was enough to make Sandy salivate. She had nearly forgotten how good her cafe's food was.

"No public spirit, you, that's your trouble." Dorie scolded. "You do make a nice breakfast, though."

"Come on, Dorie, put us out of our misery. What's happened?"

Dorie rolled her eyes as she took a bite of her sandwich, which she chewed with theatrical slowness.

"I already told you." She said finally. "There's been another murder!"

Sandy felt her stomach flip and wasn't sure whether it was with dread or adrenaline. She had wanted a peaceful return to Waterfell Tweed, but if there had been a murder, she was curious to learn more.

"How do you know this?" Bernice asked. "I watched the

news this morning and there was nothing mentioned on there."

"I have a man on the inside." Dorie said with a shrug.

"A man on the inside? Seriously?"

"Oh yes. And it's not my Jim, before you ask. I wouldn't compromise him by sharing the secrets he tells me."

Sandy stifled a laugh. She was sure that Jim Slaughter, Dorie's son, told her nothing at all about his work as a police constable.

"Okay, what do you know?" Sandy asked.

"Well, it's Hugo Tate."

"Who?" Sandy and Bernice asked in unison.

"Hugo Tate, the lawyer's husband."

"Ingrid Tate's husband?" Sandy asked. She thought back to her earlier brush with the law, and how the immaculate but cold and distant lawyer had assisted her.

"Precisely." Dorie confirmed.

"What happened to him? How much do you know?" Sandy asked. She felt her curiosity grow. She had never even heard the man's name before, but she knew immediately that she would do all she could to find his killer.

"He was shot, apparently. Happened last night. They're keeping it quiet for some reason."

"Why would they keep a murder quiet?" Bernice asked.

"I don't know." Sandy admitted.

"Well?" Dorie asked. "Are you going to investigate?"

"I don't know, Dorie, they might already have the killer. That could be why they're not rushing to make it public news."

Dorie pulled a face. "Rubbish. We've seen what a pig's ear DC Sullivan has made of the murders, he's not man enough for the job. And my Jim, well, they're threatened by him, aren't they? Won't let him work his magic, so we're stuck with you, Sandy. You're the best hope we've got."

Sandy swallowed. "Let's see what news comes out, yeah? I don't know enough to do anything yet."

"Don't be so silly!" Dorie exclaimed, as she chewed a bite of her sandwich. A splodge of red sauce fell on her chin. "You have to get started now while the evidence is fresh."

"I wouldn't know where to start." Sandy admitted.

"I think she's right." Bernice said. "If you're going to crack the case, you should start now. Go out and see what you can find out about this man."

Suddenly, Sandy's phone rang. An unfamiliar number.

"Answer it!" Dorie encouraged. "It could be DC Sullivan asking for your help."

Sandy laughed. "I doubt it, Dorie. It'll be a sales call. Double glazing or life insurance!"

The call ended and Sandy looked around the cafe. It was almost opening time and she knew that Dorie would be present most of the day, drinking mugs of tea and sharing her theory about the latest murder.

"I might go upstairs and see if there's any information about Hugo Tate online." Sandy said.

Dorie nodded frantically.

Upstairs, Sandy loaded up the computer and typed the dead man's name into an internet search.

The first result was his profile on a professional networking site. Most of his profile information was blank.

The next result appeared to be for a different gentleman with the same name.

And all of the other results appeared to be for that other person as well.

Sandy sighed and took out a notebook from the top

drawer of the counter desk. She turned to a new page and scrawled in the middle of the page, HUGO TATE.

She pictured Ingrid Tate's cool composure and wondered how she had reacted to the news that her husband had been killed.

Her phone pinged then to notify her that a voicemail had been left.

She dialled the voicemail option and listened to the four voicemails already left on the device, which were, as she had expected, all unwanted sales calls of one type or another.

The last message, though, the one left just moments before, made a shiver run down her spine.

"Sandy?" Came the urgent tone. "This is Ingrid Tate. I'm calling you from HMP Leyton Scrubs, the bastards have charged me with murder! I need to speak to you. I'll add you to my visitor list. Come as soon as you can."

3

*H*MP Leyton Scrubs sat four miles outside Waterfell Tweed, in a location only accessible by car and with nothing else around it. Anyone passing the barbed wired circumference of the prison grounds was there to attend the prison and nothing else.

Sandy had decided to take a lunch break from Books and Bakes, but she hadn't planned to drive to the prison. She had planned to drive aimlessly, with her thoughts for company, but had found herself sitting in a small public car park directly outside the prison grounds.

All of the empty cars parked there were old and weather-battered, much like her own trusty Land Rover. All of the cars except the one parked furthest from the entrance, a latest model, high-end Mercedes with a personal plate.

Sandy looked from car to car and wondered about their owners.

What would it be like to be a regular visitor there? Arriving each week, or fortnight, to visit someone special enough to keep you returning.

She shook her head and gazed out at the sprawling stone building that lay behind the wire, where she knew that around 600 male and female prisoners slept, ate, showered and tried their best to get through the endless hours that stretched before them.

The building of the prison had been opposed, but that wasn't unusual. The villagers in Waterfell Tweed and the other nearby villages and small towns opposed most new development plans. However strongly they had protested that the beautiful, rural Peak District was not appropriate for a prison, the government had disagreed and fast-tracked plans for the prison to be built and opened. Less than a year after the development proposals were first mentioned, HMP Leyton Scrubs opened its doors, welcoming security van after security van of prisoners from over-populated prisons around the country. Only the second prison in the country to house men and women, it had made the kind of national news that Waterfell Tweed didn't want to be associated with.

It hadn't all been bad news for the local villages. The prison had created a mouth-watering number of jobs and plenty of farmers in particular had, over the years, decided to give up their family businesses and retrain as prison officers. That was how new, first-generation farmers and shepherds like Gurdip had been able to make Waterfell Tweed their home.

As Sandy watched, she saw activity. A security van drove past the car park, towards the formal entrance for the prison, where entry was via a manned barrier.

More prisoners, perhaps, she thought as she watched the barrier lift and the van disappear from view into the prison grounds.

She tried to picture herself walking towards that barrier,

asking whoever was sat in the booth passing dead time whether she was in the right place as a visitor.

She couldn't picture what would happen after that.

What it would be like to walk into a prison.

She shuddered as she tried to imagine it.

She wasn't going to think her way to an answer this time, she realised, and picked up her phone.

"Cass?" She said when her best friend answered on the second ring.

"Are you okay? I've got Mrs Tillerman in for nails but I thought it might be an emergency."

"Oh, no, not really. Sorry. Listen, can you come over tonight? I need your help."

"Sure thing. I'll bring wine."

"You're the best."

"I know." Cass said. "Gotta go."

Sandy smiled as she punched in the next number.

"I really shouldn't be taking this call, if my boss found out she'd kill me." Coral said. The hustle and bustle of Books and Bakes was audible in the background.

"Very funny. Your boss wonders if you fancy some over-time tonight at her house."

"Erm..."

"I'm inviting you over. I need to talk."

"Dum, dum, dum." Coral sang out. "Sounds ominous, my favourite. I'll be there."

Sandy ended the call and then typed out a message to Tom, asking him to also join in the gathering. The three people whose opinions she valued most in the world could surely help her decide whether to get involved.

In the meantime, she wanted to get away from HMP Leyton Scrubs.

As quick as possible.

**

Tom arrived early, as always, bearing a bunch of roses and a bottle of white wine. He kissed her on both cheeks as she let him in.

"Very continental." She joked.

"Well, you know, I am an international traveller now I've been to Scotland..." He said. She tried not to stare as he pulled off his coat and scarf and hung them over her coat stand. He was so charming, so handsome. When she wasn't with him, she forgot just how special he was.

Coral arrived next, wrapped up in an enormous scarf.

"Bloomin 'eck, it's frigid out there tonight."

"They say a storm's coming, it's meant to snow." Tom called from the living room.

"Snow? It's March!" Coral exclaimed. "Hello, by the way. Nice to see you, Tom."

"And you." He said. They both appeared to be considering whether to hug, but neither of them moved towards the other and then the awkward moment passed.

"Can I get -" Sandy began, but a knock at the door interrupted her. She padded down the hallway and opened the door.

"Ooh, I'm so pleased to see you!" Cass said as she waltzed in; the same brand of wine that Tom had brought tucked under her arm. "We've not had a girls' night in too long!"

"Erm..." Sandy began, but Cass walked past her towards the living room.

"Oh, Tom, how nice that you could join. Are you staying?" Cass asked, then turned to look at Sandy. "Is he staying?"

"Yes, I need you all here. Let me get drinks and then I'll explain everything."

"Are you pregnant?" Cass asked.

"No!" Tom exclaimed. "At least, not that I..."

"No, I'm definitely not pregnant." Sandy said.

"Engaged?" Cass asked.

"Oh my gosh, Cass, could you embarrass them any more?" Coral asked. "I think it's something serious, something worrying."

"Why didn't you say?" Cass asked. She held the wine out to Sandy. "Here, get us all a glass of this."

"I've already brought some wine over." Tom said. Sandy saw Cass take a moment to clear her facial expression before she smiled at him, and silently pleaded that her best friend and boyfriend would get along.

"We might need them both tonight." Sandy said. "Give me two secs."

She escaped into the solitude of the kitchen to find The Cat staring up at her. "Come on in if you want, everyone will want to see you."

The Cat stalked past her and she was about to fist-punch the air for her masterful tone and his obedience, when instead of turning right into the living room, he turned left and climbed the staircase.

"Come on, I'll help you carry the glasses." Coral said as she appeared in the living room doorway.

Sandy passed her two glasses and followed her back in the living room, carrying the other two glasses herself.

All three of her guests watched her closely, curious to hear what was so important for her to summon the meeting.

"Okay, so how many of you have heard about Hugo Tate's murder?" Sandy asked.

Three blank faces looked back at her.

"I know the name." Coral said. "He's been killed?"

"Yesterday." Sandy said. "He was shot."

"Not again." Cass said. She took a long sip of wine. "I thought we'd gone back to being a quiet little village."

"Are you thinking of investigating?" Tom asked.

Sandy shrugged. "I wasn't going to. I'd never even heard the man's name before, and it's being kept hush-hush by the media, so I don't know where I'd start."

"Coral, who is he?"

"I can't quite remember." Coral said. She looked up and to the right as she searched her memory. "I could look into it, ask a few people. I think I've wrote articles about him before but that doesn't narrow it down much."

"He's Ingrid Tate's husband." Sandy said.

"The lawyer?"

She nodded.

"So, he was probably a professional." Cass guessed. "It was probably a business deal gone wrong."

"Professionals don't tend to shoot each other, Cass." Coral said.

Cass shrugged. "I read the papers, you'd be surprised what people do when money's at stake."

"It's awful news, Sand, but why are we all gathered here about it?" Tom asked.

"Well, I wasn't going to get involved. And then I had a phone call, from Ingrid Tate, asking for my help. It turns out, she's been charged with killing him. She's in prison. She wants me to go and see her."

"That's insane." Cass said. "You can't visit someone in prison!"

"She can, Cass, anyone can if the prisoner accepts your visit." Coral explained.

"But…" Cass started.

"Do you want to do it?" Coral asked.

Sandy took a sip of her own wine, enjoying the light-headed feeling it gave her. Her concerns seemed less serious. Her confidence increased. "I think I do."

"Well that was easy." Coral said. "Just be careful."

"I think I'll need your help." Sandy said. "You three. Are you in?"

Cass, Coral and Tom glanced at each other before returning their gazes to Sandy and each nodding their head with some reluctance.

"Coral, can you find that information about Hugo Tate?"

"I'll try." Coral said. "Who knows what state my files are in at the newspaper now. I'll give it a go."

"Okay. It's time to find a murderer."

4

*S*andy's second drive to HMP Leyton Scrubs seemed to take an eternity. Her stomach spasmed with nerves each time her car turned a corner, expecting the prison would be revealed to her. Bend after bend she navigated through the snow that had fallen in the twilight hours, but the journey was slower than it had been the week before.

Bad weather made the narrow roads treacherous, and most motorists had taken alternate routes or stayed at home. For Sandy, there were no alternate routes. She was on the prison road, nervous about what she was about to experience.

Text me when you get there safe, Coral had instructed.

Tom had offered to drive her.

Cass had said nothing, her silence deafening. Her best friend either didn't approve of her new relationship, or her visit to Ingrid, and Sandy didn't want to find out which.

Finally, four bends later than she had expected, she maneuvered around a tight bend where the road had drystone walls on both sides, to find the prison stood in the distance ahead of her. She swallowed her nerves and glanced at the clock on the car's dashboard. She'd set off early to allow for extra time given the weather, and was pleased to see she was a few minutes early.

When she'd booked the visit, the staff had been insistent that she arrive on time.

"If you're not here at that exact time, you won't go through." She had been told.

She drove down to the prison grounds and into the car park where she'd sat the week before. As before, there were a collection of cars of varying age and condition, and the new Mercedes sat furthest away from the entrance again.

She took a deep breath and climbed out of the car, locked the door and began the walk towards the barrier.

"Visitin'?" A gruff voice called out to her as she reached the barrier. She looked across at the booth, where a man in uniform sat on a swivel chair behind a glass pane, his attention momentarily diverted from the crossword puzzle in his lap to attend to her.

"Yes, am I in the right place?" She asked.

The man scowled. "Not really, love. First time, eh?"

She nodded.

"Visitors around the other side. Ya can walk it. Hurry though, they won't wait for ya."

"Thanks." Sandy said, noting the direction he gestured. She took off at the fastest pace that felt safe with the snow beginning to settle on the ground, and followed the circumference of the barbed wire fence until she reached a building that stood outside the wire. An old, decrepit playground stood next to the building's automatic doors, but nobody played on it today.

"12.15?" A large woman called to Sandy as she burst through the automatic doors.

She nodded, out of breath slightly.

"S'your lucky day, everythin's on a go slow today. Come on over." The woman said, and Sandy walked up to the counter where she stood. The woman's body was bursting out in between every button of her shirt, and her demeanour looked like that of a woman who knew how to handle trouble. "Name?"

"Sandy Shaw."

"Seriously? Cos I ain't got time for games."

Sandy felt her cheeks flush. "It really is, look."

She dug in her handbag and pulled out her purse, then retrieved her driving licence, which she passed across the countertop to the woman.

"Hmm, crazy what people'll call their kids. Seen worse in here."

"I'm here to see Ingrid Tate." Sandy explained. She'd had a lifetime of jokes about her and her sister's seaside names and wasn't affected by the comments now.

"Of course." The woman said. She typed into her computer and nodded. "Okay, stand right there and here we go, done."

"What?" Sandy asked.

"Your photo, just took your photo. You'll need to do fingerprints and then you're gonna be good to go. You know you can't take anything in there, yeah? We have lockers, you'll need a pound coin."

"I don't think I've..."

"No pound coin, you're gonna have to run back to your vehicle and leave your bag there. No unattended bags in here and no I can't lend you a pound, don't even ask." The woman said. She stopped her typing for a moment and looked at Sandy. "I think you're gonna want to have a good look for a pound coin."

Sandy unzipped her purse and, to her surprise, found several coins, including a pound coin. "I've got one."

"I'm delighted for you." The woman said, in a tone that was not quite sarcastic enough to have her complained about. "Fingerprints."

Sandy had never given her fingerprints before, and was surprised by how distressing she found the procedure. The formality of it, the very essence of her person being recorded on a government system, spooked her.

"And you're done." The woman said. "You're gonna go through those doors right there, you'll find your group in security. Do as you're told, and you'll be just fine. Don't forget your bag on the way out."

Sandy smiled her thanks and walked over to the far wall, which was covered with small lockers. She opened the door to one and stuffed her handbag in, locked it up with her pound coin, and then left the reception area via another automatic door, which took her outside. She was within the prison grounds now, behind the barbed wire. The tall walls of the main prison stood just a few feet ahead of her, down a spongy path with another deserted playground on the right.

Children must come here, Sandy realised, and as soon as the thought hit her she realised how obvious it was. Of course children came here. The prison must be full of mothers, grandfathers and cousins. People who had children on the outside who would miss their presence enough to come to this place to see them. Did the children have to give fingerprints, Sandy wondered, then forced the thought out of her mind.

She entered the main prison complex via another automatic door, and immediately felt the energy of the place. A nervous, unpredictable energy that left everyone on high alert. As if anything could happen at a moment's notice.

"Join the line!" A female officer called as Sandy entered the security room. Four other visitors were in a queue waiting to go through airport-style security, with six other people stood after the security check waiting with a different officer.

Sandy filed in as she was told to. The officers had batons and their expressions were serious. The walls of the room, chipped and faded, were covered with warnings about the consequences of smuggling things into jail. Sandy stared straight ahead, desperate to avoid eye contact with everyone, and shuffled forward when the others did.

Finally, it was her turn to walk through the security check. The alarm sounded and she was instructed to stand on a box with her arms out to each side, while a female officer with bad skin and a slight moustache patted her down for a physical check.

"You're okay." She said, and gestured for Sandy to join the other visitors.

The officer stationed with them led them out of the security check area, into a narrow corridor with a locked door at the far end. When all of them were in the corridor, he locked the door behind them, and only then did he unlock the next door and allow them to file out of the building and across another, longer path towards a huge building that appeared to be the main body of the prison. Sandy had thought the last building was the prison itself, and the sense of being lost in locked buildings, each one bigger than the last, disoriented her.

The officer unlocked the door they reached, allowed them all to file in, and then locked the door behind them. A metal gate, painted white, stood in front of them, and the officer unlocked that and then locked it after them. It seemed that prison life was all about locking and unlocking doors. Sandy had never suffered with claustrophobia but began to worry that she might.

"Straight down to the desk." The officer said. The group followed his orders and walked down the narrow corridor. Sandy, at the back, watched the others. They were an ordinary group of people. She could have passed any one of them on the street and had no idea they had someone gone from their life. One woman, dressed in a suit, sobbed quietly as they walked down the corridor, while a couple of teenage boys near the front of the crowd chatted and laughed to each other.

An elderly man who walked painfully in front of her stopped suddenly, and she instinctively took hold of his arm in case he fell.

"Are you okay?" She asked.

He smiled up at her gratefully, his eyes grey and watery. "It gets harder every time."

She bit her lip and nodded at him, having no words that could comfort him.

"Bill, need a hand?" The officer asked from the front of the group. The old man straightened his spine and shook his head.

"No sir, I'm okay now." He said, proud.

"Nearly there." The officer said. He led them to another locked door, which Sandy could see opened into the visiting room. Low tables, fixed to the ground, with one chair in front and two chairs behind, also fixed to the ground, filled the room. Nobody sat at the desks.

It was fifteen minutes into the visiting hour already, a clock on the wall revealed.

"Here we go folks, you know the drill. Take a seat at a desk and wait. Do not move when the inmates arrive, do not physically touch the inmates, do not raise your voices.

Remain seated throughout the visit or you'll have the visit shut down for everyone. If you need help, raise your hand."

He unlocked and opened the door, which Sandy noted was heavy and reinforced, and the visitors filed in one by one.

Sandy took a seat at a table close to the door. She was about to sit down with a woman charged with murder. It felt surreal.

After minutes of waiting, the door at the far end of the room opened and a prison guard led in around ten visitors. The women searched the room for the face they were expecting and made their ways separately to the table where their visitor waited. Sandy watched the subtle, muted reunions. A few inmates smiled, others showed no emotion at all.

In the middle of the line, eyes alert, posture impeccable, was Ingrid Tate. Her eyes landed on Sandy and gave one nod of recognition and made her way to sit across from her.

"You look well." Sandy said. An inane thing to say in the circumstances, but true. Ingrid somehow appeared as cool and confident, as well put together, on the inside as she had on the outside.

"Of course, dear." Ingrid said. "One simply has mountains of time to pluck eyebrows and suchlike in here. No tweezers, of course, to make the job easier."

Sandy gave a small outtake of breath, meant to signal a laugh but in such a subtle way that it wouldn't be inappropriate.

"We don't have long." Ingrid said, with a glance to the wall clock.

"I was here on time, it's..."

"Visits never start on time, don't worry." Ingrid said. "But I don't have time for pleasantries. I didn't when I was sitting on that side of the table and I certainly don't now. I need your help, Sandy."

"But why me?"

"I know how you've been solving the murders. The police might like to pretend it's all their own work, but I know what's really going on. It seems like you're the only person who can prove I didn't do this."

"Surely you're the best person, Ingrid, with your skills?" Sandy asked.

"Ha! I don't find killers, Sandy, I get killers let off."

A shiver ran down Sandy's spine as Ingrid's words sank in.

"Oh, come on. I know it doesn't sound nice, but that's a lawyer's job. I don't ask my clients if they've really done it. They tell me they're innocent and I work on that. So, actually solving a case, finding the real killer, I've got no more clue about that than anyone else."

"I didn't even know your husband, though."

"Well, I don't see why that matters." Ingrid said.

"For all of the other murders, I've had some kind of link. This one, I mean, it hasn't even hit the news. I wouldn't know where to start."

"Well, what do you want to know?"

"Erm, I guess I don't know that either."

"Shall I just tell you a little about him? Would that help?"

Sandy shrugged. She felt out of her depth, and the woman in the suit, who was meeting with a young woman who looked like she must be her daughter, continued to sob audibly.

Ingrid noticed Sandy glance across to them. "First visit. Always the worst."

"I'm sorry you're in here, Ingrid." Sandy said. "Is it awful?"

"Awful?!" Ingrid asked with some amusement. "This will be the best PR I've ever had, as long as you crack the case of course. I couldn't pay for all of the media attention I'll be getting soon!"

"But if you're found guilty..."

"I know, I know. I know better than most. We don't have time for that. Sit comfortably and let me tell you a little about my husband. Hugo was a dreamer. Delusional, really..."

Sandy gulped. "Stop. I'd like to get the facts first, not the emotion. I do want to help you. You helped me, and I know I owe you for that."

"Spoken like a true gang member, that should help you no ends!" Ingrid exclaimed.

"Gang member?"

"I'm joking, dear, goodness, I know you're not a gang girl. But the real killer, well, they were in a gang."

"A gang? Well surely that rules you out right away, I mean, it's pretty obvious you're not a gang member!"

"Oh Sandy, they don't think I did it."

"I'm confused, why are you in here?"

"Look at these nails." Ingrid said, and she held up her long, slim hands to show her manicured nails. "They don't think I pulled the trigger. They think I ordered the hit."

5

*S*andy was pleased to return to the normality of Books and Bakes the following day. She slept in and arrived just before opening time, to the heady scent of cinnamon rolls and chocolate fudge cake. Comfort foods.

"You're too good." She said to Bernice as she poked her head into the kitchen. Bernice gave her a slow, cautious smile. "What's up?"

"We had a weird call earlier." Bernice said, as she returned the morning's freshly cleaned pots and pans to the cupboards.

"Was it another call for the vet's?" Sandy asked. "I really need to get that sorted."

"No, not that. A man asking if we'd mind TV cameras coming later to do a feature on us."

Sandy clasped her hands over her mouth and forced herself not to descend into excited shrieking, which she knew Bernice wouldn't approve of. "A TV crew? You're kidding? This is amazing!" Sandy exclaimed.

"Hmm." Bernice said with an eyebrow raised.

"What did you tell them? Please tell me you said yes."

"I said it's not really for me to say but I thought the boss would agree, so they'll be here this afternoon." Bernice said, head buried in the fridge longer than it needed to be. "I'll stay back here when they come."

"Oh, Bernice, you're such an important part of this place, you should be out front showing yourself off."

Bernice closed the fridge door and glared at Sandy, arms folded across her chest. "I've got zero interest in showing myself off. I know how big this could be for you, Sand, and I really hope it goes well. But I can't be involved in it."

Sandy nodded. The thought of appearing on camera didn't fill her with excitement, but the extra attention the shop would get did. She'd push through her nerves. "Will they want an interview?"

Bernice shrugged. "I couldn't say. Oh, the Hugo Tate news is out, by the way."

"It is?" Sandy asked, eyes wide.

Bernice nodded. "Saw it online this morning."

"Thanks, Bernice." Sandy said. "I'm gonna go upstairs."

She took the stairs two at a time and took a seat behind the book shop counter, where she turned on the computer and loaded up an online news site. The murder wasn't remarkable enough to have made the national news, but when she did a search for Hugo Tate, she found an article from the closest city's newspaper.

LOCAL TEACHER KILLED IN GANG HIT the headline reads.

A teacher? Sandy had imagined him as being a lawyer, like Ingrid. She clicked onto the full story, where a photo of Hugo Tate stood below the main headline. He was bald-headed, bespectacled and entirely plain-looking. Sandy could have passed him in the street without even realising a person had been there.

Ingrid was so immaculately presented, so regal. It was hard to imagine the two as a couple.

She continued reading.

Hugo Tate, teacher at The Grove primary school, was said to be respected and liked by teachers and students alike. He was killed in a shooting that is being treated as an ordered gang hit, and is survived by his brother and partner.

Sandy clicked through to another article covering the death. This one featured a video of Hugo Tate speaking to the local news about the building of a sensory garden at the school. He stuttered throughout the interview, and adjusted his glasses with a frequency that bordered on obsession.

The text below the video was a much more in-depth article about his life.

Mr Tate campaigned for additional funds to be released to The Grove primary school and was instrumental in the school transforming its OFSTED ratings within two years. While never taking a formal leadership role at the school, Mr Tate was a core member of the staff and will be sorely missed. His legacy includes the Early Worms Reading Club, the annual trip to the Natural History Museum in London, and, of course, the sensory garden.

Mr Tate, the ex-husband of renowned solicitor Ingrid Tate, who has been charged with his murder, is survived by his brother Marshall.

"Oh my." Sandy said.

"Everythin' alright, lady?" Derrick called. He stood a few feet away from her, a large box in his hands.

"Derrick! You made me jump." Sandy said as she composed herself. "What's that?"

"New stock's arrived, I said I'd help the guys bring it up." Derrick said. He walked past her and into the storage room, where he placed the box on the floor. "Are you sure you're okay?"

"Yeah, yeah... I just got some surprising news." Sandy said, with a smile. She had thought that Ingrid and Hugo were a couple, married, cohabiting. Her being his ex-wife gave her such an obvious motive it was almost cliched, and yet most cliches became that because they were true so often.

Three burly men appeared out of the lift, all dragging a loaded pulley stacked high with boxes of books.

"Where'd ya want 'em?" One called across to Sandy.

"In here, mate." Derrick replied, gesturing to the storage room. Sandy watched the men work and tried to put thoughts of Hugo Tate to the back of her mind. The new stock arriving was exciting, and she wanted to enjoy it. Each time she blinked, however, she saw the bespectacled, nervous face of Hugo Tate. A man who had campaigned tirelessly for a primary school. Who on Earth would want such a man dead?

She sighed and returned downstairs, where she found the cafe almost half-full.

Felix Bartholomow, the elderly man renting Dorie's cottage, sat at a table close to the counter, resplendent in a suit, tie and flat cap. He beamed when he saw Sandy and attempted to stand, despite him needing a cane to support his weight.

"Sit down Felix, I'm not the queen." She teased, although his chivalry flattered her. "How are you doing? Looking very suave."

"I've got a date." He confessed, his eyes bright.

"Fabulous!" Sandy exclaimed. "Who's the lucky lady?"

"She's just about to walk in." Felix said with a wink. Sandy turned to see Dorie Slaughter push the door open, looking just as unique and impressive in her leopard print fur coat, a dozen brightly coloured necklaces bobbing around her neck.

"I don't know why you insist on paying your rent in cash, Felix." Dorie cursed as she pulled out the seat opposite him. "I'm a busy woman, I can't be coming down here every month to see you. Bacon sandwich, Sandy, and a mug of tea, since you're just standing around wasting time."

Sandy looked at Felix, who grinned at her with perfectly white false teeth.

"You look as beautiful as the first sunrise of the year." Felix said.

Dorie blushed. "Well, yes, and I do prefer that tie to the awful spotted one. You know that."

"I remembered." Felix said. "It's so good to see you again, Dorie."

"I hope you're keeping my place clean. I know what you bachelors are like. Toothpaste left all over the sink to crust!"

"Make an honest man of me, eh?" He asked.

"Get away with yer, you silly old sod." Dorie said, but Sandy saw a smile flash at the corners of her mouth.

"Have you seen those two?" She asked Coral, who was stood behind the counter gazing at the drinks machine. "Dorie and Felix? They're so cute."

"I don't know how I feel about it to be honest, when a woman my gran's age has a better love life than me." Coral admitted.

"What are you trying to make?"

"Latte, for the Welsh chap. I've already thrown two cappuccinos away. Don't know how much longer he'll wait."

Sandy turned and looked out at the tables. She recognised everyone apart from a man sat alone on one of the tables furthest away. He was well-dressed, with a shiny bald head and a perfectly round, protruding stomach. If his patience was wearing thin, he gave no sign of it. His gaze was fixed on looking out of the window.

"I'll do it." Sandy said. She demonstrated, yet again, how a latte was made by pressing the *latte* button on the large machine, although in Coral's defence, the text on lots of the buttons was worn off or hard to read. The machine would need replacing soon, an expense Sandy had budgeted for.

She carried the drink across to the Welsh man, who gazed straight past her and flashed an enormous smile at someone behind her. Sandy turned and saw the most plastic-perfect woman she had ever set eyes on. The woman was like a caricature, tiny waist, enormous breasts, big blonde hair, large blue eyes, and a tiny nose.

"My darling!" The man cried, in an effeminate voice that suggested she wasn't his darling in that sense.

The woman met Sandy's gaze and smiled. "Do I order at the counter?"

"I can take your order, what would you like?"

"Black coffee, please. Nothing to eat." She said, to Sandy's relief. Sandy wasn't sure she could have handled this woman with perfect proportions sitting and eating cake while all Sandy had to go was look at a picture in a recipe book to gain a few pounds.

"I'll bring it over." Sandy said. She returned to the counter and met Coral's gaze. "Can you make a black coffee for Barbie?"

"Meow!" Coral said, with a laugh.

Sandy felt her cheeks flush. "Sorry, that was really mean of me."

"She's stunning." Coral breathed. Sandy turned and saw that a general hush had fallen over the cafe as everyone attempted to take surreptitious glances at the blond beauty. Sandy retreated into the kitchen, where Bernice was sticking a knife into a tray of a dozen jacket potatoes to check their progress. She was about to tell Bernice about the beautiful woman in the cafe, but an excited cry rang out before she could say a word. Bernice looked at her and shrugged, and Sandy returned out front.

A young, ginger man with a TV camera on his shoulder stood in the doorway, while a smartly-dressed man with a microphone fixed to his blazer addressed the customers. "If you can stay calm, please, while we film. The shrieks don't come across too great on TV."

"Ah, hello." Sandy said as she strode across to the TV presenter. "I'm Sandy Shaw, the owner. I was expecting you."

"Brill." He said. "Thanks for letting us film here. So, we're doing a piece on the murder, you knew him, yeah?"

"What?" Sandy asked.

"The murder? Hugo Tate?"

"No, I didn't know him." Sandy admitted. "I thought this was a piece about my business."

The presenter looked at the cameraman, who shrugged. "Maybe next time. Hot news now is Hugo Tate. You can't do any kind of interview about him?"

"Well, no, like I say, I never met him." Sandy said.

"Perhaps I could help?" The Welsh man called, his lilting voice attracting the presenter's attention. The Welsh man rose to his feet and held out a hand to the presenter. "Marshall Tate. Hugo is - was - my little brother."

Sandy stifled a gasp.

"Mr Tate, I'm sorry for your loss." The presenter said, the feeling behind the words not quite reaching his voice. "We want to do a feature about your brother. He sounds like a great man."

Marshall Tate took a quick intake of breath and nodded. "He was indeed."

"Would you speak to us today?" The presenter asked.

"Of course." Marshall agreed readily. "I want the whole world to know what a special man Hugo was."

The presenter and cameraman spent ten minutes chatting with Marshall at the back of the cafe. Ten minutes that Sandy watched them from behind the counter.

"Ask them to mention the name of this place on air." Coral suggested.

"I can't do that." Sandy said.

Coral shrugged. "I would. Bloomin' cheeky if you ask me, using this place."

"Okay, we're here live in Waterfell Tweed with Mr Marshall Tate, brother of the late Hugo Tate who was tragically killed. Marshall, thank you for speaking to us today. Can you start by telling us a little about Hugo?"

Marshall's eyes were already damp and the question triggered more tears from him. "He was a beautiful soul. I was his big brother, always there to be the leader, to do things first, and yet Hugo managed to do more, much more, in his life than I have in mine. He overtook me in every way, and I was delighted to sit back and watch him. He was a good, good man."

"Do you have any idea why someone would have wanted to hurt him?"

"I have no idea. My brother was a good man."

"His ex-wife Ingrid has been charged with his murder. Do you know her well?"

"No." Hugo said, and a dark cloud transformed his face. "I would say that my relationship with my brother changed when he settled down with Ingrid. It was less encouraged for us to be close. And, it is my deepest regret, that we didn't have time to rekindle that bond before he was... he was..."

Sandy looked away as gut-wrenching sobs took over Marshall's body.

"You seem confident that you would have been able to grow closer again?"

"Oh absolutely. We had a lifelong bond. And Hugo had moved on, his new partner was much more, well... accommodating." Marshall said. His gaze fell on the blond woman, who watched him closely and swallowed.

6

*S*andy sat on her settee that night, with The Cat on her left, and Tom on her right. A tub of popcorn sat on her lap.

"This is why I'm not a size two like Hugo Tate's new woman." Sandy said, as she grabbed another handful of popcorn and ate it piece by piece.

"You're perfect as you are." Tom said, which was the right answer but one she couldn't believe he meant. She wondered what Tom's reaction would have been if he'd seen the woman in the cafe that day.

"Oh, Tom." She sighed. "I don't know where to start with this case."

"Well, now you know Ingrid's his ex, surely that changes things?" He said.

"Not really." She said. "Wives kill husbands, ex-wives kill husbands. It's a crime of passion either way. It's not like she had zero motive as his wife."

"True." Tom said. "Wow, I love it when you talk romantic to me."

She laughed and flicked a piece of popcorn at him. It

bounced off his chest and flew back past her, before it landed on The Cat's fur. The Cat opened an eye and hissed at Tom.

"Oops, sorry Catkins." Tom said.

"Don't patronise The Cat, Tom. I can't be held responsible for what he might do to you." Tom laughed. "Let's just relax and not think about Hugo tonight, yeah?"

"Sounds perfect." Sandy said. She put the popcorn on the coffee table and nuzzled into Tom's side, enjoying the warmth of him. He had messaged her earlier and asked if he could come over and watch mindless reality shows with her, and she had grinned like a fool at the mundanity of the suggestion before responding with a resounding yes.

"Oh, we need to change the channel." Sandy realised. The programme they had been watching, about people voting each other off of a coach holiday around Europe, had finished. "Where's the remote?"

"I think you had it." Tom said.

She moved away from him and looked around the settee for the long, black remote control.

"You know my mum always called it the oopie-doopie?"

"What?" Sandy asked. She pulled a face in amusement.

"Yep. She'd always be goin' around the house asking, 'where's me oopie-doopie'. Good times." Tom said.

The conversation was interrupted by the news beginning on the TV.

Further arrest made in the murder of Hugo Tate. Domingo Cavali, a criminal with links to The Blood Ties, a gang thought to have a national presence, has been charged with murder and remanded into custody. Cavali is no stranger to the legal world, with previous convictions for violence and robbery. Most recently, he made the news when he was found not guilty of an armed robbery despite overwhelming evidence against him. It is thought that Tate's murder was a hit ordered by his ex-wife, Ingrid Tate, who is also charged with murder.

"Wow." Sandy said. The television showed a Hispanic man with a neat moustache and cropped beard, his head shaved.

"Cavali... I know that name." Tom said.

"Really? You know this guy?"

"No, not him. I know a... geeze what's his name? Donovan! Donovan Cavali."

"Think they're related?" Sandy asked, her wind whirring with ideas.

Tom shrugged. "I have no idea. I'm not about to ask him."

"Well, who is he? How do you know him?"

"He's a delivery driver for the brewery. I only see him to say hello to, if I take the delivery. He has this name badge on, and it's a full name one, and he's the only one who delivers to us, has been for years, so I made a point of memorising his name so I could greet him by name." Tom said. Memorising a delivery driver's name was such a generous thing to do, and it didn't surprise Sandy at all to learn that it was the kind of thing Tom did. "I know he likes a pint but never drinks on shift. Some of them do, ya know, which is worrying because I never believe we're the only pub they have a drink in and those trucks are weapons. He always says he'll have to pop in after shift one day, but he never has."

"Does he look like this guy?" Sandy asked.

Tom stared at the TV, screwed his nose up in concentration. "A little, I guess. Same skin tone. My guy's got a rounder face, I'd say. And hair. Dark hair."

"I need to speak to your guy." Sandy said. Tom sighed. "When's he due to deliver next?"

"I don't know about this, Sand. He might have nothing to do with this Domingo guy."

"Tom, trust me." Sandy urged. "I know what I'm doing. I'll ask him without him even realising what I'm doing."

Tom wasn't convinced. "And if he is related? And the whole family have got gang links? This is a whole other level of murder, Sandy. You heard - a national gang. You don't want to upset these people."

Sandy sighed. "Fine."

**

When Sandy walked into The Tweed public house the next day, she could tell by the stunned look on Tom's face that she had guessed right about Donovan Cavali's next delivery day. She had kept a close eye on the street all morning until a brewery lorry drove past. She knew that The Tweed would have several deliveries, and that Donovan Cavali wouldn't be the driver for all of them, but figured it was worth a try.

"What are you doing here?" He asked as he poured a pint for an old man sitting at the bar.

"I came to see your face." Sandy said. The white lie slipped out of her mouth easier than she had expected.

Tom cocked his head and raised his eyebrows at her. "And the truth?"

"I'll get an orange juice, please." Sandy said, to dodge the question. The old man at the bar looked from her to Tom and took his pint to enjoy in peace at a booth table.

"You're too sneaky for your own good, Miss Shaw." Tom said.

She grinned at him, although her insides danced with nerves.

The door burst open then and Donovan Cavali walked in, pulling a trolley with three casks of ale on. He was quite obviously related to Domingo. His skin was, as Tom had said, lighter, more Sahara sand than Domingo's caramel. His face was more full, hinting at a home-life that involved good cooking, his skin dotted with moles and freckles.

He kept his head down as he walked in, and Sandy noted the concern on Tom's face.

"All okay, Don?" He asked.

Donovan glanced up at him and nodded.

"Mention it." Sandy whispered. Tom looked at her, panicked, but nodded.

"Don, I saw the news last night." He began.

Donovan stopped walking and propped the trolley up so it remained in place on its own. He met Tom's gaze but said nothing.

"The Cavali guy, I don't know if he's related to you but, well, must be rough for you if he is."

Donovan nodded. "Finally. Finally someone's had the decency to mention it to my face."

His voice was accent-free, his words choked on the emotion behind them.

"I'm really sorry, buddy." Tom said. He was so natural, so at ease with this man he barely knew but considered a friend. Sandy was proud of the man he was.

"My brother." Donovan explained. He shook his head, as if in disbelief about the whole situation. "Only a kid."

"I'm so sorry." Sandy said. "I'm Sandy, by the way. I'm Tom's partner."

Donovan reached out his arm and shook Sandy's arm in a half-hearted way.

"The media are saying it was a hit ordered by someone else." Sandy. said. "Do you know who that might have been?"

Donovan looked at her, as if his vision was distorted. He tried to focus on her face. "We move in different worlds. I haven't seen him for a long time."

"Because of the things he was into?" Sandy pressed.

"He lived with me, for a while. Caught him selling dope in my garden. Had to tell him to go, man, I got kids, ya know? I can't have them around that stuff."

"It's not your fault, Don." Tom said. "Come and have a sit down, let me get you a coffee."

Donovan moved to the bar stools and obediently sat at one. Sandy noted the black scrawls on his knuckles, and Donovan noted her noting them. "Got out years ago. Not the life for me."

"The Blood Ties?" She asked.

He snorted in response. "Nah, nah, they're big time. I joined this little group, tryin'a play like a big shot. I was young and dumb. Had this mess done, realised straightaway it was a mistake. Got them to cover it up before I even left the place - said, just scribble over it all, I can't go home with that on me. I was in that gang less than a day."

"What happened to Domingo?" Sandy asked.

"Thought he'd do better than me. Started off running drugs, took over a patch. He wasn't into no gang life. Only joined a few weeks ago. I think they offered him money."

"Why would they do that?" Sandy asked. "Is that common?"

"Not really. He was riding high after getting off the armed robbery charge."

"I heard a bit about that." Sandy said. Tom placed a cup

of coffee in front of Donovan. He picked it up, hands shaking, and took a sip of the scalding liquid.

"She got him off, you know?" Donovan said.

"Who?"

"Ingrid Tate." He said, with a sad shake of his head. "I guess they think she came knocking for the favour to be repaid."

Sandy considered his words as a chill ran down her spine. She had found Ingrid to be cold and detached, but could she be that calculated?

"If I wanted to get to the bottom of what happened, to help your brother, where should I start?"

"Well, don't waste any time tryin'a speak to him. He'll feed you a load a lies. Nah, you wanna know the truth, go to the Pink Flamingo."

"The Pink Flamingo?" Sandy asked. "What's that?"

Donovan sneered at her. "Lady, you don't know what that place is, you should probably keep your nose outta this business."

7

The Pink Flamingo was a non-descript building in the middle of an industrial estate just outside of Waterfell Tweed. It had no windows and the door was solid metal. A large bruiser of a man stood guard outside the door. A neon sign, with the name and a flamingo, flashed above the door.

Sandy clutched Tom's hand as he parked up opposite in the car park of a closed carpet shop.

"Sure you want to do this?" He asked.

"I'm sure."

They walked to the door hand in hand, with the agreement that Tom would do the talking. The bruiser looked them up and down and made no move to open the door for them.

"Open?" Tom asked. Sandy heard his voice waver with nerves and hoped the bruiser wouldn't.

"Is she comin' in or workin'?" The bruiser asked, with a look in Sandy's direction that she didn't appreciate.

"We're together." Tom said. "Got some winnings to spend."

The bruiser nodded and opened the door. Tom led the way and Sandy stayed close to him, not letting go of his hand.

The Pink Flamingo was sticky floors, cigarette smoke despite the smoking ban, and men. A bar stood at the far wall, and a small man sat on a bar stool with a woman in a bright pink leotard and impossibly high heels draped on his lap. She laughed too loud at something he said, but when he made a move towards her face with his hand, she slapped his hand away and jumped off his knee.

She met Sandy's gaze for a moment, and Sandy saw tiredness in her eyes.

"Crystal!" A man's voice shouted and the woman shimmied away out of sight.

Sandy glanced up at Tom, who continued looking straight ahead but squeezed her hand in reassurance.

They approached the bar, but before they reached it, music blared out from behind them. They both turned to see a stage, and a row of scantily-clad women walk out across it.

"Oh no." Sandy murmured.

The women were of varying ages, the eldest appeared to be around fifty. The youngest, playing on her age, wore her hair in pigtails. There were five including the pink leotard woman, who appeared suddenly alert in a way that suggested a recent substance hit.

"This is awful." Sandy said. She had never been to a strip club before, or an exotic dance club as The Pink Flamingo claimed to be, but she had imagined them to be glamorous places full of beautiful women and rich men. The women appeared to be bored and jaded by their work and while most had slim stomachs and breasts that looked fake, their faces looked mean and life-beaten.

The men, who all gazed at the stage with interest, made a sadder sight than the women. One, who sat as close as possible to the stage and was closely watched by a bruiser near his table, had a sad comb-over and held his wallet in his hand. His eyes were fixated on one of the women in particular, the only one who could be described as curvy. She wore a bright red wig, deep red lipstick, and a red mini-skirt that covered exactly as much as it was intended to and not an inch more.

The redhead, aware of his focus, made eye contact with every other man in the audience and 'danced' for them, but ignored him. Gradually, he opened his wallet, causing her to glance in his direction, and then pulled out a £50 note, at which point she left the stage and, having seized the note and tucked it inside the stockings she wore, danced up close to him.

Sandy glanced up at Tom. His cheeks were bright red, his facial expression like a terrified animal who has been trapped and can't figure out a way to escape.

Finally, the song ended, and the women left the stage. Nobody applauded.

"Well, that was something." Tom said.

"You can tick it off your bucket list now." Sandy said.

"How do you know I'm not here every Saturday night?" He asked.

She laughed. "You were more stunned than I was, Tom Nelson. I'm pretty sure we're both newbies to the exotic dance circuit."

"Can I help you two?" A man asked. He was short with a fabulous moustache.

"Just about to get a drink." Tom said.

"I'd rather you didn't." He said. "You're making the girls uncomfortable. You're not pigs?"

"Pigs?" Tom asked.

"No, we're not police." Sandy said. "Just a regular couple looking for a fun evening."

The man eyed her, unconvinced. "I'm Tony Morton, I run this place. You stand around like that while another song's on, I'll get Tiny to escort you off the premises."

"Of course." Sandy said. "I'm sorry, we were just enjoying the dance. We didn't mean to make anyone uncomfortable. Maybe we could apologise?"

"To the girls?" Tony asked, stunned.

Sandy nodded.

"You want their attention, you pay for it."

"Oh, yes, of course. Thank you." Sandy said.

Tony walked away, looking back at them once before disappearing into the darkness behind the stage.

"He's a happy chappy." Tom said.

"You can't blame him." Sandy said. "I can't count how many rules this place is breaking. Where's Jim Slaughter when you need him, hey?"

Tom laughed. "I can't imagine Dorie would let Jim in a place like this, even if it was for work."

"True. That must be why they're still open." Sandy agreed. They giggled as they stood at the bar waiting for a barmaid to appear. The wall behind the bar overflowed with layer on top of layer of photographs of beautiful women. Women dancing, women in various states of undress, women sat on men's laps, women holding fistfuls of money. And, in the centre, was one photo bigger than the rest. "Oh my, Tom, look."

"What?" He asked. She gestured towards the beautiful blond in the large picture. The photo showed her sideways, dressed in a bra, her stomach perfectly flat, lips plumped, eyes sparkling under heavy spider-lashes.

"That one there, she was in the cafe. She was Hugo Tate's new partner."

Tom looked at her in surprise. "Seriously?"

Sandy nodded and read the name scrawled on the bottom of the photo. "Heavenli Bodie? That can't be her real name."

"Brilliant stage name for this gig." Tom said.

"Hmm." Sandy said in agreement. "Maybe she isn't a dumb blond then. I wonder what she saw in Hugo? I wonder how they met?"

Tom gazed at the photo. "She works here, you could ask her yourself."

"I didn't see her in the dance." Sandy said as a woman appeared behind the bar. She was younger and more attractive than most of the women who had been on the stage, but her expression revealed a weariness she was surely too young to understand.

"Yeah?" She asked.

"We were just admiring the pictures. Heavenli Bodie - when does she come out?"

The girl turned to look at the picture, as if she needed to remember which woman Heavenli was. "She don't work here no more."

"Oh, that's a shame. Is she at another club?" Sandy asked.

The girl rolled her eyes. "You'd have to ask me dad. Are you wanting a drink? You can't stay if you don't drink."

"Yes, yes, we'll get two lemonades."

"Lemonades." The girl repeated, then looked around the bar, ducking down to look on lower shelves. "Dunno if we've got lemonades. I can do you a pint each?"

"That'll be fine." Tom said, with a smile towards Sandy.

"So, your dad, is that Tony?" Sandy asked. The question seemed to stump the girl.

"I just call him dad." She said, after a moment's thinking.

"When's the next dance?" Tom asked.

"Every seven minutes. Here you go, that's £18."

"Eighteen pounds?!" Tom exclaimed.

"It's fine, here you go. Keep the change." Sandy said, handing a £20 note to the girl. She eyed Tom. "If you want to come to nice places, you have to expect to pay more."

He kept a straight face and they found a table as far from the stage as possible.

"Let's get out of here before the next song, yeah?" He asked.

Sandy nodded. "I can't see Tony Morton opening up any more. I wonder why Donovan told us to come here."

"Speak of the devil." Tom whispered.

"Right, what's your problem?" Tony Morton shouted. He stormed towards them from the bar. The girl who had served them craned her neck to watch him.

"Whoa!" Tom said. He stood up and placed his arms up. "We don't want any trouble, we're just enjoying a drink."

"You've been asking too many questions." Tony said. His face was red in temper, perspiration sticking to the messy fringe on his forehead. "What's the story?"

Sandy took a deep breath. "I was hoping to see Heavenli dance, that's all."

"Well weren't we all, eh?" Tony said. "She's not 'ere and she ain't coming back."

"Your daughter said." Sandy explained. "It's a shame, I heard she was a really good dancer."

Tony snorted. "She was the best this place's ever seen. You should'a seen it on a good night. She'd fill the place. You tell 'em Heavenli's on a Friday, they'd be queuing out the doors. Pigs'd turn up to close us down, see she were on and stay to watch. But she got her head screwed and now I'm screwed!"

"What do you mean, got her head screwed? Is she in trouble?"

"Fell in love with a customer, din't she? Bloody brain-boiled woman. There's one rule you don't break and that's it. She could've had another five years, ten years even. Bloody waste."

"Can't she dance if she's in a relationship?"

"It's not the relationship is it, although the men get jealous. Especially the men who meet them here, cos they think the next customer who comes in'll steal them like they bloody stole'em from me. But nah, Heavenli, she was head-strong, she woulda stayed if it weren't for the baby."

"Baby?" Sandy squeaked.

"The slim uns show first, always. With a chubby girl, you've got a few months she can hide it. Heavenli, nah, soon as the deed's done, it's bloody obvious to look at her. That's her career ruined."

Sandy gazed at Tony. "Why are you telling us all this?"

"You want to know about her, know about her. Ain't no secret."

"You must be really annoyed, I mean, if she was your best girl. You must be mad with her."

"Her? She's a woman, she can't help it. Women are like that, you'll know I'm right. You hear the right lines and you're in love, ain't nothing you can do about it. I don't blame her. I blame him. He'd got a clever tongue. Coming in here night after night, buying her time, spends it talking to her - get that! Talking to her. Don't lay a finger on her. Tells her she's too special to be here. Wants to whisk her away. And I mean, you've seen him, he's nothing to look at. She's light years out of his league and he knows it. So as soon as he gets her, he makes sure she gets pregnant. Traps her. Traps her in a life she never wanted. It's him I'm mad at."

Sandy glanced at Tom. Tony Morton was panting, his diatribe causing him to be out of breath.

"Do you keep in touch with her? To look out for her?" Sandy asked, but Tony shook his head and laughed in response.

"Enough." Tony said. "You're not pigs but you're up to summat. Finish your drinks and get out."

He looked between the two of them once more, then stalked away back to the bar, where the young girl idly blew a bubblegum bubble, until it popped.

The music began playing, a fast, erratic beat that Sandy had never heard before. The men all looked up from pints or mobile phones.

"Let's go, please." Tom begged, and Sandy nodded her agreement.

They left The Pink Flamingo and returned to the outside world, where people kept their clothes on.

ngrid's hair was off-centre as she sat across from Sandy in the visiting room. That was the only sign she was anything less than her usual, composed self. Her face was, of course, make-up free, but her skin was so clear she looked fresh-faced rather than dog-rough, as some women did when they revealed their real face after years of habitual make-up wearing.

"You're doing okay?" Sandy asked. She had arrived in better time for this second visit, but found that the processing of visitors into the prison was no quicker than it had been the previous time.

Ingrid nodded. "I saw they named Domingo. Poor boy."

"It's true you know him, then? You represented him for the armed robbery."

"Amongst other things, yes."

"They say he was guilty."

"*They* will say all sorts if you listen to them, Sandy. You know I can't discuss a client."

"Okay." Sandy accepted. "Let me ask you a general question, then. How can you do it? How can you defend someone who's guilty?"

Ingrid sighed. "People never bore of this question, sadly. It's my job to provide representation to whoever needs it, Sandy. Not the people I like. Not the people I believe. Everyone is entitled to legal representation in this country. It's my job to take instructions, and act upon them."

"But how can you defend a guilty man?"

"I can't defend a guilty man if he comes to me and tells me he's guilty and wants me to create a defence for him."

"Oh."

"But the man who comes to me, despite overwhelming evidence as to his guilt, and tells me he is not guilty? That man is entitled to his defence."

"You like Domingo?"

"I do actually, yes." Ingrid said. "I've seen his struggle."

"With the gang?"

"No, no, the gang thing is recent, if it's true at all. He's only nineteen, you know."

Sandy gulped. "I didn't know that."

"Sometimes, Sandy, a person goes so far off the rails so quickly, they can't even see the rails any more, never mind get back on them."

"You think that's what happened to Domingo?"

Ingrid shrugged. "I looked at him, when he was my client, and I could see the crossroads he stood at. Whether he was guilty or not, that case was stacked against him. He was given a second chance with that acquittal. And I could see how he could use it. His brother sat in Court. He could have gone home with that brother, asked for help, turned things around. But he chose another path."

"He could be found not guilty now too?" Sandy asked.

Ingrid shook her head. "They found him moments after

Hugo was killed. The gun was still hot in his hand. He'll plead. He'll want the recognition. The chance to get a tear tattoo."

Sandy looked at Ingrid with a blank gaze.

"It's what the gang members do when they kill someone, get a teardrop tattoo underneath their eye."

"Wow." Sandy said. "Surely that makes it easy for the police to catch murderers?"

Ingrid smiled. "There are plenty of other so-called reasons for getting the tear tattoo, and of course, anyone can get one to pretend they've committed crimes they haven't."

"I feel like this case is making me enter a whole new world. I even went to The Pink Flamingo yesterday." Sandy said. She watched Ingrid, studied her face for any sign that the name had significance to her.

"And?" Ingrid asked.

"Well, I found out on the news that you and Hugo are divorced." Sandy said. "Why didn't you tell me?"

Ingrid shrugged. "It's old news. I assume everyone knows. It wasn't a deliberate omission."

"Was it amicable?"

"Ah, Sandy, it was as amicable as it can ever be when your husband runs off with a 22 year old stripper. Whoops, my mistake. A 22 year old exotic dancer."

"You knew?"

"Yes." Ingrid said. "I knew, and I felt like the most foolish woman in the world. Hugo didn't bring much to our marriage - not looks, not money, not success, not contacts. But he did bring a certain steady quality. No matter how many murder cases I had to juggle, or how late I had to stay up working on terrorism cases, he would be there, the same old Hugo. Awfully dull. And that was what I needed, really."

"Did you know he was going to The Pink Flamingo?"

Ingrid looked down into her lap for a long time. "No. No, I didn't. I was so convinced that he was dependable, reliable, all of those awfully dull things that I knew I wasn't, that it took me by surprise when it happened. I saw them, you know."

Sandy cocked her head and waited for Ingrid to continue. The visiting hall was quieter, only four inmates had visitors.

"I had a trial collapse, a six-hander in Woolwich, frightful business it was, and I was feeling a little trauma-tised, which doesn't happen much when you've seen the things I have. I thought, I'll nip to Fortnum & Mason, buy our favourite foods, and return home and surprise Hugo. Turned out he surprised me. He wasn't expecting me home that night."

"You caught them?" Sandy asked, her mouth open in shock.

Ingrid nodded. "I caught them, sat on *my* settee, holding hands. She was wearing these ridiculous pink fleecy bottoms, a little tank top. Nothing sexy about it. I think I could've handled finding them romping in bed, but sitting down and hugging? I knew then that he'd fallen hook, line and sinker for her."

"That's awful." Sandy said. Ingrid nodded but didn't meet her gaze.

"It's also fabulous motive for murder." Ingrid said, with a smile. "But I didn't kill him."

"Who else would have the motive to hurt him?" Sandy asked. "The news is making him out to be some kind of saint."

"Oh, he was." Ingrid said. "Everything they're saying, about his devotion to that school, is entirely correct. I don't really know who else would want him dead."

"Who. You don't know who would want him dead." Sandy corrected. "You said, who else, which suggests you did want him dead."

Ingrid scoffed. "Of course I wanted him dead. I just wasn't stupid enough to act on that desire."

"Why would Domingo kill a stranger?"

"For money, of course." Ingrid said.

"But what good is money if he doesn't try to get away and he's locked up."

Ingrid shrugged. "For his family, perhaps. Or maybe he was motivated by something else - plenty of people think there is glory in taking a life, Sandy. As you said, you're entering a different world here."

Sandy sighed. "Do you think Domingo would let me visit him?"

"I can't imagine he's got a long queue of people wanting to see him, so who knows. Maybe he'll accept any visit requests he gets."

"I met his brother."

"Ah." Ingrid said. "What did that rascal have to say for himself?"

"Rascal? He told me that he tried to help Domingo, but had to kick him out after he caught him selling drugs."

Ingrid burst into a laugh. "People really do amaze me. Now, Donovan I can tell you about, he was never my client. Let's just say, there wasn't only one person selling drugs that day."

"Are you suggesting he sold his brother out?"

Ingrid shrugged. "I'm saying that he introduced his brother to a way of life, and then abandoned him. Now, Domingo pulled the trigger, and he has to face that responsibility alone. But a guiding hand from his brother might have helped before it got this far."

"That's so sad." Sandy said. "I can't imagine doing your job, Ingrid, hearing all of these sad stories. It must be heartbreaking."

"Ah, so you think I have a heart? Most people don't."

"I guess you have to protect yourself."

"Oh yes, I have been a master at that, Sandy. Protecting myself at work. Not getting too close to clients. Detaching myself from cases. Turns out, I should have been protecting myself at home. That's where the hearts really get broken."

Sandy took a deep breath. "I don't know how to say this, but I think I have to. I don't know if you know…"

"Spit it out." Ingrid scolded, then met Sandy's gaze and softened. "Look, here's a tip for you, if you're going to continue with these investigations, and you do have a flare for them, maybe you could even open a detective agency or something. Let me give you a piece of advice. You must rip the Band-Aid off, forgive the Americanism. You must tear it off, without warning, and as quick as you can. Don't you dare sit someone down, tell them you're about to pull it off, give them a talk about how sorry you are to have to pull it off, and then slowly, millimetre by millimetre, pull it off, all the time apologising for how painful it must be. No, Sandy, when you're in that situation, you tear that thing off as quick as you can. So?"

Sandy gulped and met Ingrid's gaze. "Heavenli's pregnant."

Ingrid's wild laughter attracted the attention of the prison guards who stood stationed around the room. The other visitors stopped their conversations and looked across at Ingrid. The inmates appeared less interested, their reactions dulled by time, hopelessness, or drugs.

"Ingrid? Did you hear me?"

Ingrid stopped laughing and looked straight at Sandy.

"That poor fool." She said, her eyes wild. "He couldn't have children. It's not his."

9

*S*andy had placed almost half of the new stock on the shelves, and already she could sense the bookshop returning to its previous, bulging glory. Some of the stock would have to remain in boxes until more space was made, but she wanted to make sure that the books most likely to sell were put out first.

She patrolled each aisle in turn and considered which sections had grown larger than they needed to be.

She was also entering the first spring with the increased space in the shop, and knew that the reading tastes of her customers may change as the warmer months approached.

It was almost Mother's Day, and she had created a small display area of books that she imagined mums might like. Poetry collections, skin care guides, walking tours of Britain collections. She's also ordered a small selection of Mother's Day cards, so customers could complete their Mother's Day shopping all under her roof, and she stood back and looked at the display, wondering whether to move it downstairs where more people would see it. Even the reluctant reader might have a mum who enjoyed a good book.

Yes, downstairs was much better, she decided, and packed all of the books she had selected into one of the large cardboard boxes. She took the book down in the lift and selected a bookcase that was almost empty, sat forgotten about near the staircase.

The cafe was quiet, in that mid-morning lull between breakfast and lunch. She watched Coral wipe down tables and could hear Dorie mumbling to herself.

The only other customer was a man who Sandy thought at first was a new face, until she heard his lilting voice. Marshall Tate.

"You know I had no time for either of them." He said. He sat at the table closest to Sandy, furthest away from the counter, and didn't realise he was being overheard. Sandy placed the cardboard box down on the floor, careful not to make a noise, and began to place the books on the case.

"Oh, never! Did I look okay? I'm pretty sure they got my worst side, of course." Marshall said into the phone pressed against his ear. "No, no offers yet, I don't think I'd do it anyway. Can you imagine me eating spiders in the jungle? Ha! Did you see the crying? It wasn't too much, was it? I used that onion trick, remember them teaching us that in drama school?"

Sandy listened to his every word, her face growing redder and redder as she did. Did the man have no shame?

"He's penniless, of course, but it's not always about money. You never know who's watching, I could be the perfect face for someone."

"Excuse me?" Sandy asked. She had left the books and pulled up the seat opposite Marshall. The colour drained from his face.

"I'll call you back, love, alright." He said, and ended the call. "I'm sorry, can I help you?"

"I think you owe me an explanation." Sandy said. Her face was shaking with fury. "I know you set it up so the press came here and stumbled across you, sitting here ready to give an interview."

"Ah, well, I'm..."

"Save it." Sandy said. "I've sat behind there and heard your conversation. Are you seriously hoping your brother's murder somehow launches a, what, an acting career for you?"

Marshall shrugged. "Not necessarily. I just think it's best to be open to opportunities. You never know who..."

"You said you don't like either of them. Was that Marshall and Heavenli?"

Marshall rolled his eyes. "Dear girl, if you're going to eavesdrop, do it properly. I've got no problem at all with Heavenli, apart from that silly name of course. She really needs to change that before the baby arrives."

"Who did you mean, then?"

"I don't see why you think you can interrogate me about a private conversation!" Marshall objected.

"Because right now, you look very much like a man with a motive to have ordered the hit." Sandy said, her lips pressed tightly together. "So, I'd suggest you talk."

"You must be joking. There was no love between me and Hugo, but I didn't care enough to want him dead." Marshall said with a shrug. A cup of coffee sat in front of him and he began to idly stir it with the teaspoon.

"Do you have anything to gain from his death? An inheritance, or something?"

"Absolutely nothing. The best I can hope for is a spell as a C-List celebrity doing the rounds on reality TV. Now, I'll admit to you, if those opportunities come, I'll take them. But I really would be clutching at straws if I killed him to try and get my face out there more. Don't you try to hide your face, generally, when you're a killer?"

"Not necessarily." Sandy said. "Are you telling me you came across here from Wales so you could appear on TV?"

Marshall sighed. "Look, love, it's alright for you here, as long as people like me want coffee and cake you'll be in business. Acting isn't like that. There's one role and fifteen thousand people who want it. Who knows where this opportunity could lead? A true-life drama, maybe, and I could play myself. Probably direct it as well, and give creative input about the man Hugo was."

"That's unbelievable."

"I don't claim to be the nicest person in the world." Marshall said. "Look, it is sad, but they've all been playing with fire if you ask me."

"How do you mean?"

"Well, Ingrid has enemies. People who should be out of prison and are in it. People who should be in but are out because of her."

"It wouldn't make sense for someone to try and hurt Ingrid by killing her ex-husband." Sandy said.

"Did you know they'd separated?" Marshall asked, with a raised eyebrow. "Because I didn't."

Sandy considered his question. She was hardly friends with Ingrid, but her clients wouldn't be either. It could be a possibility.

"I'm still not convinced it wasn't you." Sandy said.

Marshall pursed his lips and took out his mobile phone, which he scrolled across and then held up for Sandy to view. The image was a screenshot of his bank account, showing a minus sum balance.

"My dear, I'm afraid if I did want him dead, I'd have had

to have done it myself. I couldn't have afforded a hit man. Poor actor here, remember?"

Sandy examined the image and frowned.

"Go through the transactions if you want. You probably won't find one to Domingo Cavali, ref 'murder of my brother' but you also won't see any large cash withdrawals. Well, you won't see any large transactions at all."

Sandy met his gaze. "Okay. I'm still not happy that you've used my business as a setting for your ploy to raise your profile, so if you want to still be welcome here while you're in town, you need to tell me everything you can about your brother."

"Oh, Hugo, Hugo... he was so dull, there really isn't much to say." Marshall said. "I'm the flamboyant one, you may have noticed."

"Are you guys okay?" Coral asked, appearing at the side of their table. She eyed Sandy, checking she was okay.

"I'm just having a talk with Hugo's brother, Coral. We might be a while." Sandy said. She flashed a smile at her sister, who nodded and walked away. The door pinged to signal customers arriving.

"What was your reaction to him leaving Ingrid?" Sandy asked.

"I had no idea that had happened until I arrived here." Marshall admitted. "Hugo and me, we didn't keep in touch. Nothing in common. That's what I meant when I said I didn't have time for them. I always found him boring, and that got worse when he married Ingrid. She was so powerful, so forceful, it was like watching a cat being neutered. Or a dog, whatever. Not that he was ever the wildest tom cat in town, but he became so domesticated. Doing all the housework, bed by 9pm, it was embarrassing."

"Do you think that's why he left?"

"Well, he left because of Heavenli. Heavenli, honestly, can we call her another name? I can't keep saying that name." Marshall said with a dramatic sigh.

"What attracted him to Heavenli?"

Marshall looked at her over the top of his glasses. "She's not exactly my type, love, but even I don't need to ask that question. The bigger question is what attracted her to him?"

"I think I know the answer to that." Sandy said. "I think he showed an interest in the bit of her that nobody else did; her mind."

Marshall burst into laughter. "Yeah, righto. Hugo was a bore but he was a red-blooded male too. He wasn't thinking about her brain, trust me."

"Was it like him to have an affair, though? Because if he was seduced by a pretty girl, surely that's ten a penny."

"Are you seriously suggesting my brother and that woman had a stimulating, intellectual relationship?" Marshall asked. "Look, Hugo was always a coward. He wanted out of his marriage but he didn't dare leave, that's my guess. And Heavenli, she probably wanted out of her job but didn't have a Plan B. Almost a business arrangement, really, isn't it. He leaves his marriage without having to be more lonely than he was in it, and she gets security."

"Ingrid thought she was getting security too." Sandy said.

Marshall nodded. "Well, what a surprise my brother turned out to be."

"Are you staying around here for long?"

"I'll be here until the press dies down." Marshall said, straight-faced. "You may not approve, dear, but at least I'm honest about what I am."

Sandy nodded. "Oh, one thing, did you know Heavenli's pregnant?"

Marshall licked his lips and took a sip of the coffee. "What a mess. No, I didn't know."

"Did your brother want children?" Sandy asked. She didn't want to reveal that Hugo couldn't father children if Marshall wasn't aware of that already.

"I could probably tell you less than five things about my brother, but I know for a fact he wanted to be a father." Marshall said. His expression was serious, thoughtful, as he considered the child his brother would never know. "I teased him about it as a kid. I already knew I wouldn't be having children. I mean, you can adopt now, but back then it was unthinkable, so I just resigned myself to not liking kids. Hugo loved them, it's why he was a teacher. He wanted to be around them all the time, help them. He was the kid at school who'd volunteer to help the little ones read and stuff. Yeah, yeah, he'd have loved a babba... Done anything to get one. A shame, really, Ingrid never wanted them."

"I'm sorry." Sandy said as she realised his eyes were damp with tears.

"Not your fault, love. Not your fault. I'm absolutely here for the press, don't think I'm not. But I'm saying goodbye too. You grow up being told you should be best friends if you've got a brother, and that was never gonna be me and Hugo. But he was still the only brother I had. Parents both dead, now him, it's just me left. The family dies with me."

"Not if Heavenli has his child." Sandy said.

"Hmm." Marshall said. He gave a single nod, an unspoken shared secret held between them.

10

"*W*ow." Tom said as he handed her another book to slot into the newly created space among military history. "I can't believe his brother's cheek."

Sandy squeezed the book in and brushed a strand of hair off her face. "I dunno, I think he might have more love for Hugo than he realised."

"People are odd." Tom said. He'd taken an afternoon off work to help her finish fitting in as much of the new stock as possible. It was tiring, sweaty work, to Sandy's surprise. She wished she'd tied her hair into a ponytail. "Where next?"

"There's a spare shelf over there, we'll use that." Sandy said. Together, they lifted the large box and carried it across the shop, past a teenage boy who was flicking through the retro comic selection and chewing gum. He glanced up as they walked past, raised an eyebrow and returned to the comics. Sandy hoped he wouldn't buy any, they were comics from her own childhood. *Whizzer and Chips* had been her favourite. Her dad had walked to the newsagent each week to buy the Sunday newspaper for himself and a new comic for her and Coral to share. Coral had quickly grown bored of the comic and moved on to reading each section of the paper after their dad had finished it; her introduction to the world of journalism had been those shared Sunday mornings. Sandy had remained happy to curl up in bed and read the comic, laughing at the silly storylines.

Occasionally, on the best days, her mum would hear her laughter and appear in the bedroom doorway, a yellow rag in her hand, and tell her to move up, then climb in bed with her. She'd cuddle up close to Sandy, smelling of bleach and honey, and close her eyes. She didn't want to read the comic, she just wanted to be close to happiness.

"I've lost you again." Tom said. She shook her head to bring her back to the present. He stood close to her, his arm outstretched with books for her to add to the shelf in the right place. "You okay?"

"Sorry, I was just remembering something."

Tom grinned at her. "Looked like a nice memory from the smile on your face."

"I was thinking about my mum." Sandy said. She didn't tell people about her parents often. Her loss at such a young age made people uncomfortable.

"I'm glad you have those happy memories of her." Tom said.

"It's funny, all of the memories have a different meaning now."

"How do you mean?"

"Well." She began. "A few years ago, I'd have told you my mum was such a carefree spirit, a hippie, a dreamer. I'd have told you about her laugh and how carefree she was. But now, I think of those same memories and it's really strange, it's like I can't find her happiness."

"Do you think you're starting to forget her?" Tom asked.

His words stunned Sandy. Was that what it was?

She forced herself to bring up one of her favourite childhood memories; her and her mum dancing in the kitchen in the late afternoon. Sun poured in, distorted through the net curtain, and danced along with them. Coral wasn't there, her dad wasn't there, it was just Sandy and her mum. That's probably why it was such a fond memory.

She could remember everything, even down to the mustard colour of her mum's dress, and the way she wore her hair in a plait that started at one side of her head and worked its way around to the other side. She remembered the slight stain of pink on her mum's lips.

But as she examined the memory closer, as she searched her mum's face, as she peered into her mum's eyes, it was like examining a shell. Polished on the outside, empty within.

"No." Sandy admitted. "I remember it all. I just understand it more now. She was unhappy. I'm sure of it. I just wish I knew why."

"Lots of people are unhappy, Sand, maybe she had some bad days. You know how it is, things can get on top of you."

Sandy nodded. "I think it's more than that. I don't know, maybe I'm being silly. I just wish I could ask her."

Tom placed the books on an empty shelf and maneouvred around the box, then pulled her in close for a hug. "I'm sorry, Sand."

"Oh, it's fine." Sandy said with a forced smile. She pushed herself away from Tom and straightened her back, stretching her nervous energy out of her. "There's more urgent things to be thinking about today."

"Like sorting these books?" Tom asked with a smile. Sandy knew he had to be back at The Tweed as soon as possible, he'd left Tanya alone to look after the place but it wasn't fair for him to be absent from his business to help Sandy with her own.

"Well... and thinking of our plan with the murder case." Sandy whispered, although the teenage boy seemed to be paying no attention to them. She remembered herself at his age; adults were generally invisible to her.

"Our plan?" Tom asked.

"I thought you'd like to be more involved." Sandy said, with a shrug. "You have some good ideas."

"Hmm." Tom murmured. "Go on, where are *we* up to?"

"I confronted Marshall Tate." Sandy said. "I'm fairly sure he had nothing to do with it."

"Maybe it was Ingrid after all." Tom said. "You know, the police do get the right person sometimes."

"We can't rule her out, you're right." Sandy agreed. "Hugo left her for a younger model."

"And the younger model wasn't exactly faithful to him." Tom reminded her. "Poor guy would have been better staying where he was."

"And let that be a lesson to men everywhere..." Sandy joked, with a glare towards Tom.

He blushed and let out a nervous laugh. "It took me long enough to find happiness, Sandy, I'm not going to be giving you up, don't worry."

She grinned at his sincere words.

"Do you have any other suspects?" He asked.

"Donovan directed us to The Pink Flamingo, that has to be for Tony Morton. I think we should look into him some more."

Tom nodded.

"And..." Sandy began. "I've put in a request to go and see Domingo Cavali in prison."

"What? Are you mad?" Tom asked. His raised voice

caused the teenage boy to look up, collect his things, and move to a quieter area of the bookshop.

"Shh!" Sandy scolded. "I've requested a visit, that's all. He could refuse it, I mean I'm only a stranger."

"Sandy, I'm putting my foot down. We know for sure that he pulled the trigger and killed Hugo. I can't let you go and see him."

"Do you know what it's like visiting someone in prison?" Sandy asked. Tom looked at her but she didn't give him time to answer. "There are guards watching everything. Any sudden movements and the guards would be on him straight away. I'll be fine, honestly, and he probably won't even accept the visit."

"What do you think you're going to achieve?" Tom asked. "Do you honestly think you'll walk in there and he'll tell you who ordered the hit?"

Sandy glanced down at her shoes. "No, of course not."

"What good will it do, then?"

"I don't know." She admitted. "But I have to try."

**

Sandy returned home after dark that night.

The heat of the cottage wrapped around her as soon as she opened the door and she cursed silently for forgetting to turn it off earlier. The Cat would appreciate her poor memory, at least.

She pulled off her yellow mac and padded through to the kitchen, where she boiled the kettle and made herself a mug of mocha.

In her handbag, she had a slice of lemon and lavender

cake that she had secreted from the display case when Bernice wasn't looking. She took it out and placed it on her very best china plate, then carried the drink and cake upstairs.

"Well, pleased to see you." Sandy greeted The Cat, who lay asleep on her pillow as usual. He opened one eye as she entered the room, both eyes as she pulled back the duvet, and jumped down onto the floor as she climbed into bed. He stood, stunned, on the floor. Amazed by her cheek.

"Come on, jump back in." She encouraged, and The Cat obeyed. He curled up on her lap on top of the covers and began to purr softly.

Sandy forced herself to enjoy her cake and rich, creamy mocha while doing nothing else at all. She was always so on the go, juggling at least two different physical jobs at any time as well as another thirty or more things in her head that she must remember or give attention to.

Hugo Tate's murder had taken up time and mental energy that she didn't have to spare.

For one evening only, she would enjoy her cake, sip her drink, and stroke her pet.

The case would wait.

11

*D*omingo Cavali accepted Sandy's visit request.

That was the first surprise.

Domingo Cavali was handsome.

That was the second surprise.

He flashed her a flirtatious smile as he sat across from her, and she felt her composure leave. Not because she was attracted to him, but because she was nothing like the stern mugshot the television news was showing of him.

"Domingo, thanks for seeing me." Sandy said.

He nodded. "No idea who you are, got me curious. Who sent ya?"

"Nobody." Sandy said. "I heard about what happened on the news and thought I'd come and see you. It must be lonely in here."

He sneered at her a little. "Guessing you ain't never done time."

"No, no, I like to visit people though." Sandy said. She had dressed in her most conservative outfit and kept her face free from make-up. Her long brown hair sat in a bun. She hoped to portray the image of a stranger concerned for his soul. She knew she couldn't arouse his suspicion. "Do you like having visitors?"

"Gets me outta the cell." He said with a shrug.

"Good." Sandy said. "I'm glad to get you out of your cell. It must be so hard being in there all day and night. Are they treating you right?"

"Better than I deserve for what I did." He said. Sandy noted that his face was free of the tear-tattoo that a murderer could carry and wondered if he was remorseful.

"You look younger than on the news." Sandy said.

"Nineteen."

Sandy felt her stomach flip. "You're just a baby."

He laughed. "Whole life ahead of me, yeah yeah... I was never a baby. Things I saw, things I done, I'm in the best place."

"But don't you want a family? A partner?" Sandy asked.

Something flashed across his face but it was unreadable. He was unreadable. Hardened.

"Everyone want a killer for a husband." Domingo said. "Until they get out and then the threat gets real, know what I mean?"

"Not really." Sandy admitted.

"Love letters." He said, the words making him shake his head. "They say I'm stupid, to do that hit, but I ain't writin' to no killer saying we can be together, for real."

"Where's that accent from?" Sandy asked.

He laughed again. "It's from da streets. You ain't been there."

"No, I probably haven't." Sandy admitted. "So, it's true what they're saying? You did it?"

"Bang! You're dead!" Domingo said, as he made a gun shape with his hand and pretended to fire at Sandy. He maintained eye contact throughout and Sandy felt a chill run down her spine as she looked back into his emotionless eyes.

"Cavali, enough." A male guard called. He sprinted across to their desk and grabbed hold of Domingo, while another officer shielded Sandy.

"I think he was joking." Sandy explained. "He wasn't threatening me."

"You have no idea, lady." The guard in front of her said. When she moved away, Domingo had been dragged out of the room.

Sandy felt her body shake.

"You're gonna be fine, come on, come with me." The guard said. She led Sandy out of the visiting room into a small decompression area where she made her a sugary cup of tea and reminded her about the rules around visiting. "Next time you come, as soon as anything like that happens, you gesture for help. We're watching, but we're watching more than just you. We hadn't seen that, he could've jumped you. You remember, ok, for next time?"

Sandy nodded as she drank the sweet tea.

There wouldn't be a next time.

om sulked for the whole evening, right until Sandy said she was going back to The Pink Flamingo.

"Are you trying to send me into an early grave?" He asked, arms crossed, mouth stern. He sat on her settee, The Cat curled up asleep on his lap for once, looking like a bad guy from an action movie.

"I need to see this through, Tom." She explained. "I'm in too deep to give up now."

"What do you think you're going to do? Go in there and confront Tony Morton?"

Sandy shrugged. She didn't have the best plan laid out, that was true. "I guess I thought I'd just stake the place out for a bit. See what I see."

"Stake the place out?" Tom asked. He shook his head and closed his eyes. "Listen to yourself, Sand, it's like you're in a spy movie! But this is real life, and you don't mess with these people."

"I'll stay safe, I promise." Sandy said. "And anyway, we're just sat here not talking, I know you're unhappy with me..."

"Of course I'm unhappy! You went to see a murderer in prison. He could have hurt you!" Tom exclaimed. His voice was high with emotion and The Cat had moved away unhappily to a quieter place near the log fire.

"If you don't want me to get hurt, why don't you come with me?" Sandy offered.

Tom pursed his lips and pulled her in for a hug. He smelt of cat and fear. "Of course I'm coming. I wouldn't let you go alone."

Sandy nestled in to his firm chest and considered the options. She could stay right there, in the warmth of her cottage, with the man she loved, or she could head out in the cold to spy on an unpredictable and possibly dangerous man. But she knew which she would do, even though she wasn't sure she understood her choice. In the past, she'd been so happy with a quiet life. What had happened to her?

"Let's go then." Tom said, his words a surprise to her. He planted a kiss on the top of her head and moved out from underneath her embrace. "You won't settle until it's done."

She flashed him an apologetic smile and pulled herself up from the settee.

"One thing." He said. "Leave the mac at home."

Sandy grinned. There was nothing subtle about her bright yellow rain mac. She pulled on a black hoodie instead and assessed her reflection in the hallway mirror. "Do I look like I'm going out to do a burglary?"

Tom looked at her and smiled. "If we get arrested, I'm blaming it all on you."

**

They drove to the industrial park in silence, each distracted with nervous thoughts.

Tom found a parking space hidden around the side of another building, which gave views of the club while hiding their car from view. Once he turned the headlights off, there was no reason to imagine the car would come to anyone's attention. All of the other units looked on, shutters down, lights off. Sandy wondered how many of their owners and workers clocked off and headed straight across to The Pink Flamingo. It was almost approaching Sandy's bedtime, and The Pink Flamingo was entering its peak time.

A bouncer stood outside and a dingy, sodden, red carpet lay on the pavement outside to welcome customers. It seemed fitting, the carpet. The suggestion of glamour with the reality of something unpleasant - much like the experience inside.

Sandy had packed her home-made flapjack and a thermos of coffee, although her stomach flipped with nerves and she doubted she could face food and drink.

A steady line of men, all weather-beaten and shifty, made their way into the club, swallowed by the darkness of the entrance.

"Who knew this place was here doing such a roaring trade." Sandy said. She laughed awkwardly, the silence making her uncomfortable.

Tom's gaze was focused intensely on the club. "Recognise any of them?"

Sandy shook her head. "I don't think they're villagers, they're coming from out of town."

"Hmm." Tom said. "Tony Morton might not even be here tonight. He's the owner, isn't he? He might only pop in to show his face."

"I know." Sandy said. She'd considered that possibility.

"Or, he could be inside right now confessing to the crime, and we'd be none the wiser."

"You don't want to go in, do you?"

She shook her head. "We can't do that. They thought it was odd enough the first time."

"Phew." Tom said. His discomfort was palpable.

"I really appreciate you coming out here with me, ya know." Sandy said. She smiled at him.

"I know, baby." He said. For a moment they gazed at each other, distracted.

"Oh my… look who it is!" Sandy exclaimed as she returned her attention to the club. Tom followed her gaze.

"Is that…"

"Heavenli Bodie, the one and only." Sandy said. Heavenli stood outside the club, near a closed door. She wore a hot pink dress that hugged every inch of her and, Sandy saw, revealed the tiniest swelling of her stomach. A tiny, faded denim jacket covered her upper, but was left open to highlight her enormous bosom. Her hair sat three inches on top of her head, backcombed to within an inch of its life.

"Wow." Tom said. "What's she doing here?"

The door she was stood by opened then, and out stepped Tony Morton, wearing so much denim it looked like he had a blue jumpsuit on. He closed the door after himself and leaned against it, then looked Heavenli up and down. She held her hands out in front of her, moved her weight from one stiletto-heeled foot to the other, and gave a huge smile.

Tony was silent. While Sandy and Tom weren't close enough to overhear a conversation, they could see whether someone's lips were moving. Tony, it appeared, was entranced by Heavenli, and Heavenli seemed well aware of her effect on him.

"It's like she's cast a spell on him." Tom said.

"The power of a woman." Sandy murmured.

After a few moments, Heavenli moved closer to Tony, her body almost pressed up against his.

"Are they going to kiss?" Sandy asked, bolt upright in her seat, craning to get a better view. There was no kiss, though. Heavenli sidled as close to Tony as she could without touching him, and then whispered something in his ear.

"There's nobody near them, why's she whispering?" Tom asked.

"She's teasing him." Sandy said.

A few seconds later, Tony moved away from her. His cheeks, illuminated by the club's neon signs, were red with fury. He gesticulated wildly towards Heavenli, towards the club and the signs that hung above them.

She took a step towards him and shrugged.

Her reaction to whatever had him so annoyed caused him to go crazy. He curled his fingers into a fist and punched the metal door, leaving a dint in its shape.

"She's in trouble." Tom said. "We need to help her."

Sandy sighed, her fingers trembling. "You're right."

Tom turned on the engine and began to drive towards the club. Tony Morton was so blinded by rage he didn't respond at all. Heavenli cowered in front of the building, arms wrapped around her face to protect her from the attack she expected.

"Get in!" Sandy called to her from her open window as Tom pulled up outside the club. The smell of alcohol and sweat radiated out from either The Pink Flamingo, or Tony. A frantic beat pulsated out from the club.

Heavenli glanced up at them from behind her hand-shield, then climbed to her feet and dived into the back seat.

"Where the hell are you -" Tony shouted after them, but

he made no effort to follow them. As they drove off into the distance, Tony remained outside the club, watching in amazement.

"Are you okay?" Sandy asked. She turned around to look at Heavenli in the back seat. Her dress, Sandy realised was almost too short to be decent, and her legs were covered with bruises. "Did he hurt you?"

She shook her head and pulled a mirror compact from her handbag. To Sandy's surprise, she inspected her face, which was still immaculate make-up - war paint, to cover who knew what.

"Your legs are bruised."

"They're always bruised." Heavenli said with a shrug. Her voice was like gravel. She shivered in the back.

"Turn the heat up, Tom." Sandy commanded. "Should we get you to a hospital? You know, with the baby to think about?"

Heavenli shook her head then looked at Sandy in surprise. "Do I know you?"

"Sorry, I'm Sandy, and this is Tom. I met you briefly the other day, you came in my cafe, Books and Bakes, with Marshall."

"Oh." Heavenli said. The interaction seemed to spark no significance in her mind.

"It's okay, I'm sure your head's all over the place. I'm sorry for your loss."

"Me too." Heavenli said. "I miss him so much."

Sandy glanced away, Heavenli's raw emotion unexpected. Heavenli gazed out of the window, lost in her thoughts.

"He's a good man." Heavenli murmured.

"So I've heard." Sandy said. She assumed that Heavenli meant Hugo and couldn't bring herself to change her tense to reflect his death. Sandy remembered doing the same after her mother's death. *My mummy is...* she would tell people, and watch them glance at each other.

"Where shall we take you? Where's home for you?"

"I'm staying with friends." Heavenli said. "Drop me off anywhere and I'll make my way back."

"I'm not letting a pregnant woman get home on her own, especially after what's just happened to you." Tom said.

"I appreciate that." Heavenli said. "But, with respect, I don't know you two enough to show you where I live. There's a lot of press hanging around trying to speak to me. I'm sorry, I appreciate your coming to my rescue."

"No, it's fine. I understand." Sandy said. "Let's just find somewhere safe."

"What if I take you to The Tweed?" Tom suggested. "You can at least wait somewhere warm and safe."

"The Tweed?"

"It's a pub, my pub. It'll be warm until your lift arrives."

"Sure." Heavenli said. Her voice was quiet with exhaustion.

"Don't you know the village well?" Sandy asked.

"Not, erm, not that part." Heavenli said, which was a strange answer as the village wasn't big enough to have more than one part.

Within minutes they arrived at The Tweed and Heavenli thanked them once more before getting out of the car and teetering away on her heels. She entered the pub and walked straight to the bar, where Tanya greeted her with an amused smile.

"What shall we do now?" Sandy asked. "We shouldn't follow her in there, that'd look strange."

"Go back to yours and finish watching that programme?" Tom suggested.

Sandy nodded her agreement. They'd set out in such a rush earlier she couldn't remember if she'd even turned the television off.

"Don't you think it's strange?" Tom asked as he drove through the darkened country roads towards Sandy's cottage.

"What?"

"New widow, pregnant, out in such a seedy place dressed like that?"

Sandy considered his question. "I don't know. I guess it would be strange if I did that, but it's Heavenli's past. Wouldn't it just be like me putting on an apron and going to my workplace?"

"I don't know." Tom said. "I have a funny feeling about it. I'd love to know what she said to Tony Morton to get that reaction out of him."

"I'm more interested by the fact that she did get that reaction. God, Tom, imagine... if we hadn't been there, she could have been his second victim."

13

*I*ngrid Tate no longer looked immaculate. Her hair stood up in all directions and her eyes were bloodshot. A small scratch sat raised on her cheek.

"What happened?" Sandy asked.

Ingrid flexed her hands into fists, clenched and relaxed them, again and again. "I need to get out."

"Are you in danger?" Sandy asked.

Ingrid raised an eyebrow towards her.

"Sorry, stupid question."

"Tell me you've got news." Ingrid implored, her foot tapping on the floor to a rhythm only she could hear.

"I've ruled out Marshall Tate." Sandy said.

"Marshall? Geeze, I could have told you it wasn't him." Ingrid snapped. "That man wouldn't dare."

"Well, I had to follow the evidence, Ingrid... he turned up in the village and arranged a press conference in *my* shop." Sandy said. She was still shook up from witnessing Tony Morton's behaviour, and coming face to face with Domingo Cavali, and she'd hoped for a little more thanks from the woman she was trying to help. "Played the chief mourner role to the cameras and then I heard him saying he couldn't stand Hugo."

Ingrid flinched at her words but Sandy held her gaze and fought the instinct to apologise for her harsh words.

"Marshall's in the village?"

Sandy nodded.

"I would never have expected him to travel across here for Hugo." Ingrid said. "But he was indifferent, well, they were indifferent to each other. There was no hate between them."

"Unlike you and Hugo?" Sandy asked.

Ingrid faltered. Her mouth opened and then closed again.

"Why didn't you tell me to start with that you were divorced?" Sandy asked. She was wasting time but Ingrid's lack of thanks had annoyed her.

Ingrid sighed. "We've been through this! I wanted you to review the case and do what the police didn't bother to. I wanted you to investigate! It's such an easy arrest, isn't it, the bitter ex-wife? Lazy policing drives me insane."

"And clients who don't tell you the truth?" Sandy asked. "Do *they* drive you insane?"

Ingrid physically reacted to the words, her head jerked back and eyes opened wide. Then she flashed a large smile and laughed softly. "Touche, dear girl. Okay, no more playing games. I'll be honest with you, about everything."

Sandy waited, but Ingrid said nothing more.

"You need to ask me the questions, Sandy. I'm not just going to tell you my life story. Come on, you can do this. What's puzzling you? Which things don't make sense? Who are your leads?"

"I went to visit Domingo." Sandy blurted.

"Good!" Ingrid said, eyes wild, searching Sandy's face for emotion. "I hoped you would. Was he... okay?"

"He didn't have a tear tattoo."

"Interesting." Ingrid said. She scratched at her cheek and opened the graze, a trickle of blood welled up and she wiped it away. "Sorry, damn thing's so itchy."

Sandy pursed her lips. "I didn't ask him who ordered the hit, and now I'm wishing I had. But I didn't think he'd tell me."

"Oh, he wouldn't tell you." Ingrid said. "It's really very interesting that there's no tattoo."

"It means he didn't do it for the glory."

"Or the money."

"Money?" Sandy asked.

"You need to have a chunk of money to buy a hitman, Sandy."

"You said he might have wanted to send that money to his family. Couldn't he be sorry but still have done it for money?"

"He has no family." Ingrid said with a sigh. "Only Donovan, really, and I don't think Domingo would do something so desperate for him."

"Why else would he do it then?" Sandy asked.

Ingrid shook her head. "Fear, perhaps. If it's not money, it's power... they must have had a power over him."

Sandy continued to look at her quizzically.

"You know what I mean by power, come on, think it through! Fear, love, hate, a secret you need to keep secret..."

"Tony Morton." Sandy whispered.

"Who?"

"When I saw Donovan, he told me to go to The Pink Flamingo. Tony Morton is the owner."

"The Pink... Flamingo?" Ingrid asked, the words sparking a memory.

"Heavenli worked there." Sandy explained. "There are posters of her on the wall still. She must have been the biggest attraction that place has ever had, what with her... erm..."

"She's beautiful, you can say it." Ingrid said.

"Why would Tony Morton have power over Domingo? That's what I don't understand."

"Why would he want Hugo dead?" Ingrid asked.

"Well, my thinking is, he was angry that Heavenli left the club and blamed Hugo. Heavenli getting pregnant was probably the last straw." Sandy explained.

"Hmm." Ingrid murmured, not convinced. "Why do you think he was that bothered? Owner of a club like that, you expect the girls to come and go."

"I saw him with her. I was watching the outside of The Pink Flamingo, I don't know what I was looking for, but Heavenli turned up. There was an argument with Tony Morton, she whispered something to him, it seemed flirty to start with, and then he got angry. I had to rescue her."

"Maybe she was still refusing to go back to work?" Ingrid asked.

"Possibly. She wouldn't tell us anything, she was cagey. But I saw the way he looked at her."

"The way I guess all men look at her?" Ingrid asked.

"Pretty much." Sandy said. "It wasn't the way a concerned employer would look at an employee whose just been widowed."

"The baby could be his." Ingrid said. She covered her mouth with a long, slender hand.

"Oh my... I've been thinking the baby was Hugo's, I'd forgotten... well, that's motive! Surely?"

"Sandy." Ingrid said, her tone serious. "I think we need to take this to the police now."

"No!" Sandy objected.

"I'm putting you in danger, it's selfish of me. Let's show the professionals what you've found."

"I've found nothing." Sandy said. "You know what they're like, as far as they're concerned their case is closed. You're guilty to them. They won't take any of this seriously."

Ingrid took a deep breath. Her shoulders were crumpled into her chest, she sat low in the chair. Hopeless. "It's up to you now, I'm not going to encourage it any more."

"Ingrid, I can..."

"I've done, Sandy. Let's leave it for today." She muttered. She raised a hand and a prison guard sauntered across to her.

"What's up, Tate?"

"I feel ill, I need to go back to my cell." Ingrid said. The guard grunted and waved over another officer.

"I'll show your visitor out." The guard said. "Tate's feeling ill."

"Geeze." The second guard said. "You better not throw up on me. Already had that happen this week."

"I'll see you soon, Ingrid, okay? Look after yourself." Sandy said as she stood up.

"Goodbye, Sandy." Ingrid whispered. "Thank you for helping me."

**

Sandy emerged from the cold, impersonal prison building to what had become a bright, sunny day. The sun sat high in the sky, heat spatters warming her face as she walked along the perimeter of the compound towards her car.

"What am I not seeing?" Sandy asked herself out loud. She pictured Ingrid's beaten-down expression. How awful it must be to face the possibility of being convicted for a murder she hadn't committed.

Sandy turned around and gazed back at the prison. Visiting time had finished and other people were streaming out of the visitors' hall like ants. She watched them, fascinated by the new world she was experiencing where a portion of time each week or month had to be assigned to visiting this place.

As she opened her car door, her phone rang. *Cass.*

"Hey." She said as she sank into the driver's seat. She left the door open, enjoying the warm rays on her.

"I miss your face!" Cass said. "And Mrs Sweeney's cancelled, again, surprise surprise... so I thought I'd give you a call. You're not at the shop?"

"No, I've been to visit Ingrid, I'm just about to leave." Sandy said. The swarm of departing visitors continued to approach, their shadows tall in front of them as they transitioned from prison to the real world. "What are you going to do about Mrs Sweeney?"

Cass sighed. Sandy had told her for a while that she should take deposits from her beauty salon customers when they booked appointments, in case they cancelled at short notice. "I might just block her number so she can't book in again! Honestly, it's so annoying. Anyway, there are bigger problems I guess... I bet Ingrid's not worrying about her nails right now."

"She looks awful." Sandy admitted. "And I don't think she's safe. She's got a cut on her face. I thought she'd be ok, I thought they'd love to have a lawyer in prison to help them."

"I guess it depends how many of them she's already helped..." Cass said.

"Oh God." Sandy exclaimed. "You mean her old clients who've been sent down could be in there with her?"

"Well, it's the only prison nearby... I mean, John Moon's in there, isn't he?"

A chill ran down Sandy's spine. "Men? Men are in there too?"

She remembered John Moon's case because of how awful it had been. The media coverage had lasted months, and even through only catching parts of it here and there, Sandy had considered the man obviously guilty of the awful crimes. He pleaded not guilty and a long, drawn-out trial resulted in a jury finding him guilty after less than twenty minutes deliberating.

Ingrid had been his lawyer, and while she had had to remain silent about him as a client after the case, he had taken to writing angry letters to any newspaper or magazine who might print them, criticising her advice and work, suggesting she had known he could access 'unlimited' money and had ripped him off because of that, and even accusing her of flirting with him.

Sandy remembered Coral telling her about the crazy letters John Moon had sent in to the newspaper where she had been a journalist. Sandy had shook her head and they'd both agreed the streets were safer with him locked away.

The thought that Ingrid was under the same roof as him filled her with dread.

A raucous laugh from the group of visitors caused Sandy to look up.

"No way!" She exclaimed.

"What? What is it, Sand?" Cass asked down the phone.

"I can't believe what I'm seeing." Sandy whispered. She dropped low in her seat and watched the familiar face walk, alone at the back of the group, towards the car park. She saw the grief on their face and realised there was no risk the person would spot her as she had spotted them. They were in a world of their own, trapped in thoughts Sandy could only begin to guess.

"Sandy, you're worrying me."

"I know who ordered the hit." Sandy whispered, then ended the call.

She waited until the person climbed into the Mercedes and drove out of the car park, then closed her own car door and sat up in the seat.

She needed to make a plan to confront them.

Because she knew this person would have only one reason to visit HMP Leyton Scrubs.

14

*S*he shouldn't have come.

Dread refused to leave her as she got ready, dressing in a plain black dress, pairing it with dark tights and a pair of low heels.

She shouldn't have come. As she brushed her long mane of hair and spun it into a bun to sit high atop her head.

She shouldn't have come. As she climbed into Coral's car and allowed her sister to fill the air with inane chatter.

She shouldn't have come.

And yet, she had.

The church overflowed with faces, many of them village residents, but plenty of them shifty, unknown faces, attending for the story they could write or the stolen photograph they could sell on.

Sandy smiled towards Dorie, who sat nestled between her son Jim, and her renter Felix, an arm draped around each of them. She wore a garish purple dress and balanced a lilac beret on her head. Heavy lip liner stressed the full shape of the lips she wished she had, rather than the ones that existed on her face.

Tom was at The Tweed, preparing for the wake. Sandy had tried not to take it personally when an out of town catering company had been asked to prepare the food. She didn't want catering work, she tried to remind herself. But, still.

Coral gripped her hand as they sat down. She too must realise that it was a mistake for the two of them to be there together. Sandy pinched the top of her nose to keep the memories away. They had already sat side by side in this church too often. She let out a choke before it strangled her.

"Okay?" Coral asked.

Sandy nodded furiously, motion to remove the emotion. Coral understood; said nothing else.

As the pallbearers entered, coffin held high, Sandy took a sharp intake of breath. Surely the murdered man's body wouldn't be released for some time, months perhaps. Or was that a fiction that only occurred on TV crime shows?

Heavenli followed the coffin, dressed in a black pencil skirt and a black, lace top that hinted at the swelling of her stomach beneath. Her eyes were dark with kohl, lips sparkled under pink shimmer. The contrast was hypnotising. Even Sandy struggled to take her eyes off the beautiful widow.

Behind her walked Marshall, his skin shining with the leathery orange of a recent extended period on a sunbed. He grinned and waved at random faces in the crowd, then caught himself and wiped an invisible tear from the corner of one eye.

"Oh, no." Coral whispered, as a hoard of school children paced in next. Dressed in uniform, they filed in two by two as if they were about to board the Ark. The tallest stared straight ahead, while some of the others assessed the crowd and one began to skip. As if height revealed maturity.

"Ladies and gentlemen." Rob Fields began as the children filed in place behind him. "We welcome the children who knew Hugo Tate best. Please, take a seat as they share with us his favourite hymn."

Sandy thought of butterscotch tart, sweet and rich. Flapjacks made with diced cherries and ground almonds. Lemon trifle, layer after layer of sponge, lemon jelly, custard, lemon curd, lashings of cream. She remembered how she had once thought that blind baking meant working in the kitchen while being blindfolded. Pictured cornflake tarts, the cornflakes sitting on a bed of jam and then sprinkled with a dash of dessicated coconut.

She thought of anything and everything to distract herself from listening to those heartbroken children sing.

Coral gripped her hand, nails into flesh, and Sandy managed a smile in her direction.

"And now, let us pray for the soul of our friend Hugo. A man who did so much for our community, who was selfless and..."

Sandy filtered out the vicar's words. They were true, and false, as she imagined the platitudes given out at most funerals were.

Nobody ever gave a eulogy that revealed a person's faults, did they.

Rob Fields wouldn't go on to remind the grieving audience about the marriage Hugo had abandoned, about the death-do-us-part commitment he had made and broken.

Was the same true for her mum, Sandy wondered, the thought crashing into her. Did her own mum's funeral focus on bare platitudes instead of memorialising the woman she had really been. The thought was so unexpected, so painful, that Sandy jumped up from her seat, removed her low heels, and ran out of the church, only returning the shoes to her feet when she was safely out of the church with the door closed behind her.

She stood, for a moment, under the shelter of the entrance. The heavens had opened, crying for the loss of Hugo Tate perhaps, and Sandy had no coat. She hoped that Coral would sense her desire to be alone, and after a few moments felt safe to assume her sister wasn't going to follow her out. She began a leisurely walk around the perimeter of the village square, enjoying the rain falling on her.

When she reached The Tweed, a harried Tom glanced at her as he laid out foil platters of vol-au-vents. He did a double take. "What's happened?"

She smiled, imagining how she must look emerging from the rain. "I guess I don't always handle funerals very well."

"Oh, come here, you sweet, sweet girl." He said and pulled her in to his firm chest for a hug. She nestled into him but he jumped away. "You're soaking me! Go up and get changed."

She shrugged. "I'll be okay."

"Sandy, go, please." He instructed.

"I could help?" She offered, looking at the sealed boxes of food.

"Yes, you can. Get changed and then help. I can't believe they don't lay it all out themselves, I've seen the invoice. Heavenli must be made of money."

Sandy tutted as she walked towards the door that led to Tom's living quarters. "She should have used Books and Bakes."

"I hear their hygiene rating's a bit dodgy..." Tom teased

as she disappeared into the back. Sandy climbed the stairs and opened the door to Tom's bedroom. She had no clothes at his, but the radiators were scorching, she could feel their heat just by being in the room, so she pulled off her dress and wrapped herself in Tom's dressing gown, then draped her dress over the radiator to dry.

In the mirror, she inspected her reflection. Her make-up remained in place, a benefit of not wearing much meant there simply wasn't enough to run because of a bit of rain. She released her hair from the bun and towel dried it, patting it until it merely hinted at being damp. Tom may have a hairdryer, but she didn't know where it was kept and wasn't about to go searching.

Instead, she walked across to Tom's library, her favourite room in perhaps the whole world, and took a seat.

The phone shook in her hand as she dialled the number.

"I need to speak to DC Sullivan." Sandy told the operator. "No, I don't have his collar number."

"I have a lot of DC Sullivans, without a collar number I can't locate him." The operator said. Tired. Fed up with enquiries like this, where the caller only had partial information.

"He's based at Waterfell Tweed, I think." Sandy said, although she had seen no sign of him since before Hugo's murder. Maybe the city police had grown bored of investigating village murders. And Hugo's, well, it was different. On a bigger scale, with the gangland element of it. Maybe an ordered hit was above even DC Sullivan's head.

"I have no record of a DC Sullivan at that station."

"Well, he isn't based there usually, I think he's there now."

"I'm going to need more information, sorry." The operator said. Sorry not sorry. "A collar number, or the station they're assigned to, not the one they may be at today."

"I'll call you back." Sandy said with a deep sigh. She ended the call as the woman began her scripted farewell.

It would be down to her, then. She stood up and returned to Tom's bedroom, felt at her dress. It would do for the walk home. She could curl up in bed with The Cat and make a plan.

She dressed and emerged from Tom's room, quietly descended the stairs, hoping she could sneak out of the back exit so she wouldn't have to walk through the crowded wake.

A person stood in her path, back to Sandy, head bent in towards their shoulder.

Sandy paused. Frozen.

"I know, baby." They whispered. "I miss you too."

Sandy cleared her throat.

The phone dropped to the floor, and the person bent, gingerly, towards it.

"Let me." Sandy said. "You shouldn't strain yourself, in your condition."

Heavenli stared at her, eyes wide like the moon.

Sandy picked up the smart phone, bigger than her own purse, and placed it to her ear. So noisy. Breathing, sure, but noise too. Communal noise.

"You can call her back, Domingo." She said, and ended the call.

Heavenli cupped her tiny stomach. A reminder that despite so much being false, that was real.

"We need to talk." Sandy said. She gestured to the staircase she had just walked down, and Heavenli climbed upwards.

In the library, she took a seat by the fireplace. Sandy remained standing.

"So." Sandy said. "Does he know about the baby?"

Heavenli nodded.

"You needed Hugo out of the way. Couldn't you have just left him? Why kill him?"

Heavenli's face blanched, grey like a mushroom. "You think I killed him?"

"No, I think you ordered the hit. Domingo loves you, he wants to be with you."

"Well, that plan worked then." Heavenli said with an eye roll. She had the biggest eyes Sandy had ever seen. Eyes bigger than her waist.

"Heavenli, I'm not the police. You can tell me what happened." Sandy pleaded. "Ingrid wants to, she needs to know the truth."

Heavenli smiled. "I know."

"Tell me what you know, then."

She sighed. "Domingo and me, we go back too far. On again, off again, I wanted to settle down. Hugo was more sensible than any man I've been with. It's a crazy ride when you look like this."

"But you've made yourself look like that." Sandy said. "No disrespect."

"Some women spent tens of thousands on University, I spent it on my looks." She said with a shrug. She was smart, Sandy realised, beneath the make-up. "I knew I had to make another life for the baby."

"Hold on, you were pregnant when you…"

"Hugo knew I was pregnant, knew I wasn't with the dad." Heavenli explained. "We said we could be each other's way out. A friendship, really. He was going to help me retrain, go into beauty therapy. I guess I was there to make him brave enough to leave Ingrid."

"So, what went wrong?"

As Heavenli allowed her body to relax, she cupped her stomach with both hands. She was more pregnant than people thought, Sandy realised. A whole, growing baby tucked into her tiny frame.

"The same as always." Heavenli said. "He fell in love with me. They always do."

"You could have just left him."

"He wanted the baby." She said. "He wanted the baby more than he wanted me. He told me I'd never get custody. I'm a stripper, he's a teacher. He was going to take her."

"The baby wasn't his to take..." Sandy said.

"He made me sign something." Heavenli said, eyes wet with tears. "Kind of a, agreement, that if I died, I wanted him to keep the baby."

"So you asked Domingo to kill him?"

"No!" Heavenli exclaimed. "God, no! Is that what you think? I've used my looks my whole life, I've stripped since I was legal, but I've got no record. I've never broken the law."

Sandy paused, her theory wrong.

"I don't understand. I thought Domingo had killed him for you."

"I guess he did." Heavenli said. Soft sobs fell on to her protruding stomach.

"You're not making..."

She sighed. "It wasn't Domingo that asked for that meeting."

Sandy pursed her lips, not understanding.

Heavenli gazed at her then, and for a moment Sandy saw the woman beneath the make-up, under the false spider lashes. "It was an ordered hit, alright. It was Hugo, ordering a hit on me."

"What? He wanted you dead?"

A shiver took over the whole of Heavenli's body. "When

the baby came. I would be, erm, ran over, make it look like an accident, and then the baby would be his. He knew I wasn't going to stay, not forever."

"And if that's true, why on Earth would he go to Domingo?"

"Why not?" Heavenli asked. "He owed Ingrid a favour."

"Hugo didn't know he was the father."

Heavenli shook her head. "I guess I knew we would be together again, it made no sense to tell Hugo too much. Look, this doesn't sound good but I promise you, it was never meant to be love. He wasn't meant to fall in -" Heavenli clasped a hand over her mouth as she gasped and shifted in her seat. "It wasn't me he loved, was it? It was the baby all along. He was playing a game the whole time. He only showed an interest in me when I started to show."

Sandy pitied her, in a way. She'd been so used to men falling for her, she had believed it too easily. Believed Hugo's intentions to be those of a man besotted; a problem she could deal with.

"Argh!" She screamed then, and Sandy noticed a trickle of fluid gush onto the floor below Heavenli.

"Oh my... geeze, what's..." Sandy asked, panicked.

"It's my waters, oh God, Sandy, call an ambulance."

Sandy leapt up from the chair and dived to the top of the stairs, screamed for help, then dialled 999.

"I need an ambulance, I'm here with my... with... with someone, and her waters have just broken." Sandy explained, her words too fast.

"It's too early." Heavenli panted from the chair. "It's too early."

"Heavenli Bodie." Sandy told the operator.

"Helen." Heavenli shouted. "Helen Brown."

"Erm, I think she's saying it's actually Helen Brown." Sandy repeated. "I don't know."

"Oh God." Heavenli roared as Sandy returned to her side. She gripped both arms of the sodden chair, her face red and angry. "Tell them it's too early. I'm only 31 weeks."

"She's 31 weeks." Sandy relayed. "We're at The Tweed public house, in Waterfell Tweed. Please, come quickly, I've got no idea what to do."

The door burst open and Tom appeared, eyes wide. Tanya stood by his side and sprung into action. "Towels, Tom. Hot, clean towels. Go!"

Tom obeyed, grateful for the excuse to leave the room.

"They're saying you should breathe, Helen." Sandy said.

"Heavenli!" She raged.

"Heavenli, sorry." Sandy said. "Breathe."

The ambulance arrived within minutes, paramedics burst into the library, armed with bags of equipment, faces calm and measured.

"Alright, we're going to get you to the hospital my lovely, okay?" One of the paramedics, an older woman with a ruddy face and crazy eyebrows said in a soothing tone. "You have a friend to come with you?"

Heavenli shook her head, her eyes to the ceiling in pain.

"She's got me." Sandy said. "I'll come."

Heavenli glanced at her then, gave her a tiny smile, and Sandy knew she was telling the truth.

15

*E*sme Brown was the most beautiful baby Sandy had ever seen, and even though the list of other babies she had seen was fairly short, she raved about that fact.

With her mother's huge eyes and long dark lashes, and a hint of her father's caramel skin, and a spool of dark hair, Esme was, indeed, perfect.

Born too early but the Gods were smiling.

After so much loss, Heavenli was granted a healthy baby.

"She's perfect." Sandy said, yet again. She sat by Heavenli's hospital bed as she cradled a sleeping Esme in her arms. The baby, or the labour, had softened Heavenli somehow. Her face was paler, less contoured, her lips' natural pink softness revealed. She was dwarfed by the hospital bed, tiny and coccooned in the clinical white sheets.

"Thank you for being here." Heavenli said, then held out the infant. "Here, have a hold."

Sandy retreated, then caught her natural instinct and moved back, closer to the baby. She accepted the tiny parcel and held her, carefully, oh so carefully. There had been a time, most of her life really, when she had taken for granted the fact that one day she would birth a child and be transformed into what she considered to be the highest life role: mother.

Level 10: Unlocked!

As she held Esme Brown, the possibility of her becoming a mother seemed miniscule. An impossibility. Probably.

"You did so well." Sandy said. "After everything you've..."

"Oh, stop." Heavenli said; batted the words away with a slender hand. "No skill required in pushing a baby out."

"Hmm." Sandy considered. "I don't know about that. But you definitely need a fair amount of strength. Courage."

"The streets will give you that." Heavenli admitted.

"How many times have you visited him?" Sandy asked, her mind returned to the prison car park, the teeter of Heavenli's heels, the emotion etched on her face impossible to read.

"As often as they'd let me." Heavenli said, with a sad shrug. "I love him... and I needed to thank him."

"For killing Hugo?" Sandy asked, mouth agape.

"For saving me." Heavenli explained. "The next thug with a gun would have agreed to do it. Domingo did the only thing that could have saved my life."

"Why didn't he try to run?"

Heavenli shrugged. "He isn't proud of what he did. He isn't proud of what he is. But he's always accepted responsibility."

"The robbery?" Sandy asked. Where was his commitment to taking responsibility, then?

"Wasn't him." Heavenli said.

Sandy arched an eyebrow.

"He was with me that night." Heavenli said, then

blushed. Esme began to fuss, eyes closed like a kitten, and Sandy passed her across to Heavenli.

"Ingrid needs your help, you know. Anything you know that might convince them."

"I know." Heavenli said, with a fierce nod. "I was staying quiet for him, you know, wanted to try and save him like he saved me. He told me to speak, that's what I'll do."

Sandy nodded. "You have anyone, anyone you want me to call?"

Heavenli glanced at the clock on the wall and shook her head, then cooed to the baby. "Daddy's going to ring soon, princess, oh yes he is. Daddy rings every day, you'll see."

Sandy suddenly felt awkward sitting there, watching a woman she barely knew bond with a new baby. She shifted in the plastic seat. "I should get going."

Heavenli met her gaze and nodded. "Thanks for being here."

Sandy stood, placed a kiss on Heavenli's forehead, and then gazed down at baby Esme. She really was perfect. Sandy brushed a finger across her cheek, a stroke. "She really is perfect."

"Finally, I got something right." Heavenli said with a sad smile. Her phone began to ring and Sandy waved as she left the room, Heavenli's words of greeting dulled by the sudden newborn baby wail that Esme let out.

I'm here, daddy. She seemed to say.

I'm here.

**

It felt strange to be back in the car park without Heavenli's

Mercedes tucked away in the furthest corner. Not that there was a furthest corner. The car park was snided full, cars and vans spilled out over the grass bank as well as the pavement. Sandy surveyed the barrier for signs of life, but there was none.

No visitors entrance for her today.

She had told Bernice that she had errands to run, and Bernice had replied with a dramatic eye roll. One day, maybe she would come and go without explaining herself.

Movement, ahead.

She squinted her eyes, sure she could see something ahead.

A taxi rolled into the car park. The driver, an enormous man with a barrel belly and a nose ring, chomped on a burger as he aligned the car almost into a space. A real burger. Impressive.

Sandy climbed out of the car and walked towards the barrier.

The man in the security booth watched her, shifty. "You can't come in here."

"I know." She called back to him and moved backwards a few paces.

The shape continued to walk towards her, recognised her, burst into a grin.

"Fancy seeing you here!" Ingrid called. She looked like herself again. Well-presented, superior, detached.

"I thought you might like a lift home." Sandy explained, as the pop of a flash went off behind her. She turned to see a crowd of reporters gathered around.

"Ingrid! Ingrid! Is it true that your ex-husband was killed by the hit man he hired to kill his pregnant wife?" A voice came from the crowd.

"Ms Tate! Will you return to criminal defence work?"

"Ingrid! What do you have to say to the public who knew you were innocent all along?"

Ingrid cleared her throat and approached the reporters. "Ladies and gentlemen, thank you all for being here today. Thank you for your belief, your support, your time. I am very happy to be returning home today as an innocent woman. My message is as it has always been: it is vital that people falsely accused of horrific crimes have courageous, pro-active and fierce legal representation. I will continue to fight for my clients, as I've fought for myself, for the rest of my life."

She gave a small wave towards each of the many cameras, and then returned to Sandy's side and walked past the cackle of reporters.

"Wow... you were amazing." Sandy said. "Did you just..."

"PR, dear girl." Ingrid said, with a wink. "How do you think they knew I'd be released right around now?"

**

Sandy returned to The Tweed, the smell of fire and whisky greeted her as she walked in.

Tom sat at a booth table, nursing a glass of single malt. Coral and Cass sat next to him. All were silent.

"Well, aren't we a merry bunch?" Sandy teased.

She noted the platters of half-eaten sandwiches and quiches along the bar.

"You're back!" Tom called. He stood and reached across the booth to pull her in for an awkward hug. She grinned as she took in his scent; sweat and the lemons he sliced each evening to dump in cold glasses of cola.

"How is she?" Cass asked, eyes accentuated with purple eyeshadow.

"She's good." Sandy said. "Baby's fine. It's a miracle, the doctors said."

"Has she gone to prison?" Tom asked.

Sandy shook her head. There was so much to explain.

"You guys need to get me a glass of wine so I can bring you all up to speed." Sandy said with a laugh. Cass stood first, pleather purse shining, eager to buy. Sandy nodded her appreciation. "Thanks."

"Bet that baby's a looker." Coral said. She let out a low whistle.

"She's perfect." Sandy said, then shook her head, bored by her own repetition. "All babies are, though, aren't they?"

"Only mothers love ugly babies." Tom said.

"Tom Nelson!" Coral exclaimed with a giggle.

He shrugged. He was nervous of Coral. Lots of men were.

"Right, here we go." Cass said as she returned to the table, slid a small glass of white wine across the table towards Sandy, who picked up the glass and took a sniff. Not much of a drinker, she'd have a sip or two and then twirl the glass around in circles until she made it move too fast and some spilt, at which point people would accuse her of being drunk when she wasn't. She was famous for spilling wine. Her party trick. "Now, tell us everything."

Sandy chuckled to herself. "Like news vultures, you lot."

She relayed the news to them, watching their faces contort into oohs and aahs, surprise and shock. Concern for Heavenli.

"Maybe she could work with you." Coral quipped, but Cass remained serious.

"Maybe she could." She agreed with a deliberate nod.

"Might be just what she needs. When she's had time with baby, of course."

Sandy beamed at her best friend. "I think even the possibility would mean a lot to her. She's all alone now."

"It's tragic." Cass said. "But it's exciting too. A fresh start for her. Anything can happen now."

"That's true." Sandy agreed. Her gaze met Tom's and she felt a familiar warmth pool through her body.

She looked at him and, quite simply, felt at home.

LEMON AND LAVENDER LOAF CAKE

Ingredients:

- 2 cups all-purpose flour
    - 1 teaspoon baking powder
    - 1/2 teaspoon baking soda
    - 1/2 teaspoon salt
    - 1/4 cup vegetable oil
    - 1 cup castor sugar
    - 1 egg
    - 1 teaspoon lavender extract
    - 4 tablespoons lemon juice
    - 3/4 cup milk
    - 2 to 3 tablespoons lemon zest
    - 1/4 cup figs, chopped

Method:

1. Preheat the oven to 180C.

2. In a medium bowl, mix together the flour, lemon zest, baking powder, baking soda, and salt. Set aside.

3. In a large bowl, mix the vegetable oil and sugar. Beat in the egg. Add lavender extract and lemon juice. Fold in the figs

4. Alternate milk and the dry ingredients to the wet ingredients, mixing well after each addition. You should begin and end with the dry ingredients. Do not over mix.

5. Pour the mixture into a 9×5 loaf pan. Bake for 30-40 minutes.

6. Enjoy!

THANK YOU FOR READING

As an independent author, my success depends on readers sharing the word about my books and leaving honest reviews online.

If you enjoyed this book, please consider leaving an honest review on Amazon or GoodReads.

I know that your time is precious, and I am grateful that you chose to spend some of your time entering the world of Waterfell Tweed with me.

And to receive exclusive content and the latest news, join my VIP Reader List by visiting:

http://monamarple.com/vip-reader-list/

Click to see all of Mona Marple's cozy mystery books here.

ABOUT THE AUTHOR

Mona Marple is a mother, author and coffee enthusiast.

When she isn't busy writing a cozy mystery, she's probably curled up somewhere warm reading one.

She lives in the beautiful Peak District (where Waterfall Tweed is set in her imagination!) with her husband and daughter.

Connect with Mona:
www.MonaMarple.com
mona@monamarple.com